THE PIT of the HELL HAG

∾

About the Author

Mary Regan was born on a farm in County Derry but she has spent most of her life in Derry city. She lived for four years in England before returning to Derry where she now teaches in a primary school. Recently she was awarded a Master's Degree from the University of Ulster.

Her interests include folklore, archaeology and drama and she enjoys combining history with a touch of mystery. Donegal is one of her favourite places and she spends her summers in a caravan there. She is married with four children.

THE PIT of the HELL HAG

MARY REGAN

Book One in the Brod of Bres Trilogy

POOLBEG

Published in 1994 by
Poolbeg Press Ltd,
Knocksedan House,
123 Baldoyle Industrial Estate,
Dublin 13, Ireland

The financial assistance of the Arts Council of Northern Ireland
is gratefully acknowledged.

A catalogue record for this book is available from the British Library.

ISBN 1 85371 413 5

Cover illustration by Jane Doran,
Cover design by Poolbeg Group Services Ltd
Set by Poolbeg Group Services Ltd in Rotis Serif 10/13.5
Printed by The Guernsey Press Ltd,
Vale, Guernsey, Channel Islands.

For Morna

Contents

∽ Nastier and Nastier ∽

Nuala Deery hooked two fingers between her lips and a piercing wolf-whistle startled the swaggering footballers. The girls crouched giggling behind a parked car and watched as the boys squirmed and looked around furtively for the source of the mockery.

"Hey, Willie," called Lisa McCarron, "I've seen better legs on a table."

To the delight of the three tormentors, Wee Willie Clements blushed and stumbled, his scrawny knees knocked together and he went sprawling into Battler Doherty's broad back.

"What are you at, Willie?" growled Battler as he untangled himself from Willie's arms and legs. "Don't let them three witches get to you." Then he shouted in the direction of the parked car, "I know who yez are. Gawn home and play with your dolls."

"We'd rather watch all you action men get pulverised," shouted Aileen Kennedy but the boys had already disappeared through the gate and into the sports field.

"What do think then? Will we go to the match or not?" asked Nuala.

"Dunno," mumbled Aileen.

"Might be a bit of talent there," offered Lisa

hopefully. Nuala rolled her eyes dramatically.

"What talent?" she asked scornfully. "Sure we know what our school has to offer and I don't think there'll be any film stars on the other team."

"What'll we do then?" asked Aileen. There was silence as the three girls shuffled aimlessly along the main street of Drumenny village looking for excitement. There was none to be found.

"Suppose we might as well go," decided Nuala. "There's nothing else to do." The other two nodded in agreement. They knew all along that they would end up at the match but that didn't stop them from hoping that some better way of passing a Saturday afternoon would turn up.

Aileen stopped outside the chemist shop. "I'd need to go in and say where I'm going," she said hesitantly. "I won't be a minute."

She caught the look that Lisa threw to Nuala. It was a smirk more than a look and it didn't really come as a surprise to Aileen; Lisa had a habit of doing that sort of thing. When Aileen was on the receiving end of Lisa's ridicule she felt hurt and humiliated but when someone else was the victim she was often an uneasy co-conspirator. There was something about Lisa. Aileen could not put her hand on her heart and say in all truthfulness that she liked her but she wanted her for a friend. Everyone wanted Lisa McCarron for a friend.

Aileen knew her friends thought she was a bit of a baby, always having to say where she was going. They didn't understand. It was all right for them. They had whole families but Aileen and her mother had only each other to worry about.

She pushed open the shop door and then stood still.

The shop seemed to be empty but Aileen knew that it never was. A murmur of low voices drifted from behind a set of shelves; one was light and musical, the other deep and gruff. Then a high girlish laugh rang out and Aileen felt hot anger surging through her body. She was aware that the door had opened again and that Nuala and Lisa were now standing beside her. They nudged each other and tittered loudly. There was silence from behind the shelves, then her mother coughed and said, "Well if you give the cows a good dose twice a day they should be all right."

The gruff voice mumbled something and then a sheepish Tom Scroggy shambled into view and pushed past the prying eyes and out into the street. A second later Claire Kennedy appeared with flushed cheeks and sparkling eyes.

"Aileen, love," she said breathlessly, "I didn't hear you come in."

"I just came to tell you I'm going to the match," Aileen answered flatly, "but I don't suppose you would have been worried about me anyway." Then she turned on her heel and led the way to the street.

"They were snoggin'!" crowed Nuala once they were outside.

"They were not!" answered Aileen hotly and she could feel tears stinging the backs of her eyes.

"They were so!" retorted Nuala.

"He must have awful sick cows," said Lisa slyly. "He's been into the chemist's every Saturday afternoon for the past month, hasn't he?"

"I wouldn't know," replied Aileen, her temper beginning to rumble.

"Well, it must be some invisible cure he got," said

Lisa triumphantly, "for he left with nothing – his two hands were the one length."

In desperation, Aileen tried to get the subject off Tom Scroggy and her mother.

"If we don't hurry up we'll be late for the match," she said. "The band's stopped playing so they must be getting ready to kick-off."

For a minute she thought she had succeeded but then fate took a hand in extending her torture. Out of a door on the far side of the street came a small spare figure.

"There's your future step-granny!" howled Lisa. This was going to be more fun than a boring football match.

Aileen's heart sank. Ever since she could remember, Aggie Scroggy had been an oddity around Drumenny. She lived with her son on a lonely farm in the mountains and only came into the village once a month to do her bits of shopping. The quaint clothes she wore belonged to the last century and Aggie kept herself to herself. She was friendly enough to the villagers but generally she did her business quickly and had no small-talk. When Aileen was younger she used to think Aggie Scroggy was a witch and even now she kept her distance from the old woman.

"Come on," declared Lisa taking the two girls firmly by the elbows. "Let's see what she's up to. Maybe it's time you got to know her better, Aileen." She propelled them across the road and began following Aggie Scroggy up the long street.

Aileen could not bear to think what Lisa McCarron might do or say next so she decided to take matters into her own hands. She rushed ahead of the others and caught up with the old woman. Then she very deliberately and very forcefully bumped into her, scattering her basket and its contents all over the footpath. There wasn't much in the basket, just ordinary groceries. A large bag of flour crashed into the gutter and split open spilling its contents all over the road. A jar of salad cream splintered and splattered Aggie Scroggy's shoes with yellow blobs. A passing mongrel couldn't believe his luck as he scampered off with a packet of sausages.

"Oh dear, I'm very sorry," said Aileen and she took the basket from the unprotesting old woman and began to retrieve the scattered groceries. She replaced a dripping bottle of washing-up liquid in the basket and then scooped up the dirty flour and piled it on top. She reached the basket back to Aggie and looked her straight in the eye daring her to say anything. She was met by a strong gaze that neither flinched nor accused. The pale blue eyes bored into Aileen and there was something unfathomable in their expression.

"Thank you very much," said Aggie in a mild voice as she accepted the basket and its messy contents. "I'm sure it was an accident." She continued her journey down the street trailing drifts of flour in her wake. Aileen stood and watched as Aggie climbed into her son's battered car and then the pair of them drove off.

"That was class!" hooted Lisa admiringly. "I was sure she would scream at you or something."

"Maybe she'll go home and put a curse on you," Nuala speculated gleefully.

"Don't be stupid," snapped Aileen. "Well, are we going to the match or not?"

She should have been delighted at Lisa McCarron's approval but somehow she wasn't. She felt mean and ugly.

The match wasn't up to much and Aileen didn't want to hang around after it. She went home and tried to watch television but there was too much on her mind. There couldn't be anything between Tom Scroggy and her mother, she told herself. Claire Kennedy was young and beautiful and Tom Scroggy was old and awkward and just as odd as his mother.

Her last thoughts before dropping off to sleep that night were of Aggie Scroggy. She didn't like what she had done to the old woman. Maybe she *would* put a curse on her.

❧ An Odd Duck ❧

Seven weeks later Aileen Kennedy was sitting hunched and miserable at her desk in Drumenny School. The classroom door opened and her heart sank. Lambeg stood there and beside him was what could only be a new pupil. There was one empty place in the classroom and, unfortunately, it was the other half of Aileen's desk. The only bit of peace she now had was about to be shattered.

"I have a new boy for you, Mrs McCloskey," boomed Lambeg. The headmaster's real name was Mr Quinn but his nickname had been given to him several generations of children ago and had stuck so well that even the adults in the village called him Lambeg. The Lambeg is a drum – a big, round, very, very loud drum. The ferocity of its boom is supposed to strike fear deep into the hearts of the enemy. That is how Mr Quinn earned his nickname. He too was big, round and very, very loud but he struck fear into the heart of absolutely no one.

The newcomer hid behind the bulk of Lambeg – but not for long.

"Come out here, sir, and meet your fate."

The reluctant boy was pushed into the open space at the front of the classroom.

"Drumenny School provides the best education in these islands," Lambeg informed the quaking boy in his ear-splitting thunderclap of a voice. "It's not often we get new recruits into the leavers' class, but better late than never. Even a short spell with Mrs Mac has been known to work miracles. Am I right or am I right, Mrs Mac? Heh-heh, huh?"

Mrs McCloskey blushed and bloomed under the compliment even though she hated to be called 'Mrs Mac.'

"Well, I'll leave you to get on with it then." Lambeg retreated, the sonic boom of his voice following him right down the corridor until his office door closed on it.

There was silence in the room for a few seconds and then the murmurs and sniggers began. Aileen began to feel sorry for the boy. He was in for a rough time of it. Everything about him told her that. He was small, his hair was neatly parted and flattened and he wore a regulation school uniform of well-pressed grey trousers, grey jumper, white shirt and striped tie. Drumenny School had no regulation uniform and the very fashion conscious eleven-year-olds would just go to war on this newcomer. He would be someone new to taunt. Aileen brightened as this idea occurred to her and her hopes rocketed. Perhaps now that they had a new victim to torture they would leave her alone . . . Then her hopes crashed back down again into her baseball boots. He was going to sit beside her and so there was little chance of being ignored.

"Well now," began Mrs McCloskey as she surveyed her charge. She was really very annoyed at Mr Quinn. He had dumped this new pupil in her lap without a scrap of information and she already had thirty-five ticking time-bombs packed into the small classroom.

"Suppose you tell us something about yourself?"

All eyes were on the unfortunate boy. He stood there, burdened with a school bag as big as himself but he didn't say a word. Mrs McCloskey sighed. The class was getting very restless. She would need to get this interruption seated at a desk as quickly as possible so that she could get back to division of fractions.

"Well, as you are so shy, perhaps you would just tell us your name?"

A low mumble came from the boy.

"We can't hear you, dear, you will have to speak up."

"Robin Drake."

Even Mrs Mac was shocked into silence. The voice was strong, though shaky, but the accent was decidedly English. The class were not very good on English accents and to them he sounded just like the royal family. The teacher knew then that the rest of the school year was going to seem like a decade. At least the Halloween break was coming up.

After the short disbelieving silence came the raucous outburst of merriment. An English Wally with a daft name! This was pure heaven to the bored class.

It was Battler Doherty who started the quacking but it spread quickly. The call was taken up by the boys first but, anxious not to be left out, the girls soon followed. The duck noises started low but built up to a screeching crescendo that threatened Mrs McCloskey's precarious hold on the control of her classroom.

"Whwhshhhsplatttt!"

The long wooden meter ruler skited off the broad back of the teacher's desk, slamming the class into silence.

"That is quite enough of that nonsense, if you don't mind!" stormed the teacher; her neck was bright red and throbbing with anger.

"Ah, Robin," she said when the quacking had stopped, "you just sit down there beside Aileen – move over Aileen and make room for Robin. I'm afraid you will find yourself a bit at sea at present but if you will just listen for the moment we will sort you out eventually . . . "

Mrs McCloskey rattled on, glad that the class had not picked up her stupid reference to the sea, and Robin Drake shuffled towards Aileen. She made as much room as she could for him without falling out of the desk herself. She hadn't joined in the quacking but that didn't mean she was deliriously happy to have him sharing her space.

"Now," said Mrs McCloskey, "after that disgraceful exhibition I think we had better do some work on attitudes to others . . . "

There followed a long sermon on sharing and caring and making room for other people during which Battler Doherty made flapping wing gestures at Ronan McCafferty and Willie Clements quacked silently to Lisa McCarron.

"We will now spend some time in silence just taking a good hard look inside ourselves," concluded the harassed teacher. "I want us all to think of a time when we failed – failed completely to show a caring attitude to those around us – in the street or classroom, the playground and even in our homes. When you have finished thinking, I want you to write about it and I want you to be honest."

For a long time Aileen sat staring at the page in her

exercise book. It was shiny clean and very empty. Pale blue lines stretched across the snowy plain waiting for her sprawly untamed writing. Around the room heads were bent, some slumped right down into the crooks of elbows, and pencils were working; long elegant pencils with precision pointed leads wrote daintily and short chewed stubs with blunted tips worked wearily. Here and there faces scrunched and frowned as straining minds sought to capture sliddery ideas.

Directly across the aisle from Aileen's table Lisa McCarron chose another pencil from her jammed electric blue desk tidy. Lisa had everything – a fistful of felt-tipped pens, rainbow coloured giant paper clips, fancy racing car pencil sharpeners and a biro that wrote in six different inks. Nobody borrowed from Lisa McCarron.

Aileen was caught looking. Lisa smirked, lowered her spiral permed head on to an expensive pink shell-suited elbow and began to write.

"She'll have it read out too," thought Aileen. "*And* she'll blush and enjoy every minute of it. But she won't write about how she and Nuala Deery have teamed up with Battler Doherty, Wee Willie Clements and Ronan McCafferty to rule the class and make my life a misery."

Aileen wasn't going to write the real truth either. Just like everyone else in the class she would fill her page with some tale about skiving the dish washing, not making cups of tea, forgetting to bring in the turf and grabbing the best bun on the plate. She lowered her miserable head and began to write. A movement to her left caught her attention and without turning her head she took a quick squint through the corner of her eye. Robin Drake looked forlorn.

And indeed Robin was feeling far from happy. He had dreaded coming to this school and so far it was even worse than he had imagined. He was totally miserable and he looked it. Aileen felt a twinge of sympathy. Then she closed the new boy out of her thoughts. She had troubles enough of her own.

The journey home was the worst part of the day. The yellow and white striped school bus was dubbed the Banana Bus by the disrespectful passengers but to Aileen it was a torture chamber. When she climbed on board she was surprised to see Robin Drake staring disconsolately out of a window. Where the English boy lived was of little interest to Aileen but it had to be somewhere outside the village if he was getting the bus.

As usual, the Battler Gang crammed themselves on to the long back seat to rule the Banana Bus with fist and fear. Battler himself came waddling up the centre aisle of the bus flapping his arms and quacking hysterically. The other children cheered and quacked in chorus.

Aileen slid into an empty seat near the front among the infants and the lower juniors and hoped that nobody would notice her.

"The 'Alien' has landed!" screeched Wee Willie Clements, and all was as it had been for weeks and weeks, back to the day her mother had announced her marriage to Tom Scroggy and Aileen's life had changed completely.

"Why don't you sit in beside Chookie Birdie there and give him a squeeze," shouted Nuala Deery.

"Birds of a feather . . . " chimed Lisa McCarron and the bus exploded in rowdy laughter.

Robin Drake had been given his nickname. It wasn't irreverent but respectful like the headmaster's, nor was it inherited from a long line of past 'Battlers', all built like Finn Mac Cumhaill; it was hurtful and meant to be so. Just like Aileen's. 'Alien' was not only a corruption of her name, it was what she had become – an outsider, something different and weird.

"Come on Scroggy, why don't you turn round and give him a big loud one."

This time it was her other nickname they used. At the beginning she used to shout hotly, "My name is Aileen Kennedy!" but now she said nothing. She found it was better if she pretended she didn't hear. But Alien Scroggy she had become and she hated it.

The bus began its usual journey through the outskirts of Drumenny before striking north to run parallel to the wide mouth of the River Foyle and up into the wild country where Aileen now lived since her mother's marriage. Usually her torture eased as the children got off in dribs and drabs and she had the bus to herself for the last few miles to Cloughderg. Today she discovered, with an unpleasant shock, that this was not to be. After the last passenger had left, Robin Drake was still on the bus.

Cloughderg is a wild and lonely stretch of the country where high-ridged mountains plunge in spectacular swoops into the dark waters of Lough Foyle just where it meets the turbulent North Atlantic. Nobody at the school lived as far out as Aileen so where was this newcomer going? Did he even know that himself? The bus came to a final halt at the foot of

her lane and Aileen jumped down on to the road. She
could hear Robin Drake's footsteps behind her. She
turned into the lane and began the walk that dipped
and climbed and took her away from any contact with
school and its gangs and tauntings, towards the cause
of all her troubles. Still the footsteps followed.

The lane wove its way between high fuchsia hedges
and down the middle ran a tuft of grass like a Mohican
haircut. Once the lane had served a small fishing
community but now the three fishermen's cottages lay
empty and it provided the only link between the
outside world and two dwellings. One was Scroggy's
scrap of a mountain farm and the other belonged to
Hugh Bradley. Hugh was the 'fixer' for the entire area
including Drumenny village. He fixed everything from
cots to combine harvesters but his special genius lay in
reconditioning anything electrical. He lived by himself
and as he spent most of his time tinkering in his shed
Aileen had only seen him once or twice. Surely Robin
Drake was not going there?

Pretending to ignore the footsteps behind her Aileen
hurried on but she was listening. She passed the
overgrown track that led to the derelict cottages and
still the footsteps followed. At Bradleys' fork she
listened even more intently as the crunch of the
footsteps grew fainter. He had gone towards Hugh
Bradley's! What on earth was that English Wally doing
out here in a lonely house with an old man?

Around the last corner and there was the back door
of her house. She stubbornly refused to call it home.
The kitchen was empty and sparkling clean as usual. A
glass of milk and a plate of buttered scones were left
for her on the yellow checked cloth that covered the

large kitchen table. The wag-at-the-wall clock ticked steadily in the silence.

The door into the hall opened and Aileen turned but the smile on her face stiffened. The woman hesitated when she saw Aileen, then she came a little further into the kitchen but she still held on to the door handle. She was a thin wisp of a woman with a body as fragile as the lacy remains of a juice-drained leaf. Her hair was snow white and neatly turned and twisted into a roll along the nape of her neck. The woman was Aggie Scroggy.

The forget-me-not blue eyes were the old woman's most startling feature. They were set wide apart in a face curiously unlined and youthful for a woman of her years. The skin on the small face was delicate, almost transparent, and was stretched taut over high, firm cheeks. Aggie was dressed in her usual grey skirt that almost tipped her ankles and a buttoned-up cardigan. A pink blouse-collar and a flower-sprigged apron added the only hint of colour to the uniform. The distinctive scent of cinnamon lozenges always surrounded Aggie Scroggy.

"There's a bite to eat on the table," said Aggie in her low murmur.

Aileen lowered her eyes from the disturbing gaze. "Where's my mother?" she asked coldly.

"She's taking the tea to the field," answered Aggie. "Tom's working at the potatoes. Why don't you go up there? It's still warm enough for October."

∽ The Two-in-One ∽

After draining the ice-cold milk in one gulp and grabbing one of the buns off the plate, Aileen threw her schoolbag under the stairs and went out the back door again. But she didn't go towards the gate leading to the pocket handkerchief fields that clung to the side of the mountain. Instead she took the path that dropped in a natural staircase of rock slabs towards the shore.

A fringe of grass sprinkled with withered sea-pinks softened the last drop to the beach. It was a harsh beach of shingle and shells and seaweed-covered rocks that rolled in undulating humps to meet the waters of Lough Foyle. Today those waters were calm and sun sprinkled, but a storm had raged in the night and the wild roar of the pounding waves had disturbed Aileen's sleep.

There were plenty of sandy beaches near Cloughderg but Aileen loved this spot. Here were discoveries to be made and mysteries to solve. Under every well-thatched rock lurked whole new worlds to be wondered at and then left in peace. It was a world that changed with every incoming tide. The dark pools of briny water were Aileen's happy hunting ground. Endless hours were spent fishing out crabs and shrimps and searching whelk shells for their hermit lodgers. She never disturbed the hermit crabs; nobody knew better than Aileen what it was like to be taken from a well-loved home.

Daily she combed the stretches of coarse shelly gravel for treasure. She had found it too! Her bedroom was filled with scavenged trove. She had a fig box from Morocco painted with palm trees and exotic veiled ladies, a wooden cigar case decorated with hot-poker work and shards of soft smoky glass in hazy shades of blue and green. On her table sat a sea-scoured driftwood sculpture that was twisted and grotesque but still strangely beautiful. This was her sea harvest and this bleak beach her favourite place in the whole world. It could only be reached by the steep path from the house and so belonged to Aileen alone.

Today she did not want to poke through the rubbish on the tideline or fish in rock pools, she wanted to go to her Brooding Rock to nurse her sores. The Brooding Rock was designed by nature to be a comfortable armchair and a protection from driving rain and prying eyes. Once folded in its broad arms, Aileen could shut out the world and sink into blissful daydreams.

As she was scrambling over the slithery rocks towards her refuge she slipped and then steadied herself by grabbing a piece of loose seaweed. The weed came away in her hand and there, sitting meekly in a dark crevice, she found a small object. It had probably been washed up during the storm, she decided, and as it looked interesting she shoved it into the pocket of her jeans.

When she was settled into her Brooding Rock, Aileen withdrew the object from her pocket. She scraped the mossy slime away from the hard white stone and found a perfect little statue a bit longer than her middle finger. A lovely face smiled serenely up at Aileen and as she marvelled at its beauty all the bitter anger that had been choking her for weeks melted magically away. Then she turned the statue over and it all came flooding back again! An ugly little face scowled up at her disturbing her deeply and causing her to shiver. It was a two-faced statue. Two tiny figures were fused back to back in one piece of sculpture. At the tip of the fused heads was a small hole, big enough to string a cord through.

Quickly Aileen turned back to the beautiful face and she cradled the little statue in her cupped hands. Beneath her feet the waves shushed gently on the pebbles and far out in the smooth sun-burnished water a seal bobbed and dived for fish. A trawler chugged towards the shore at the far side of the Lough trailing in its wake a flock of hungry seagulls. She felt relaxed and at peace, almost happy.

At that moment a stone came whizzing past her head, swooped low over the water and gave three little skips before disappearing beneath the waves. Aileen sat staring in shocked disbelief at the spot where the stone had disappeared. Someone had invaded her private territory! Another stone came whizzing past Aileen's Brooding Rock. She leapt to her feet and stormed out of her hidey-hole and there on the grassy bank stood Robin Drake. She could see that she had startled him.

"H-h-hallo," he muttered smiling a little worried smile. Aileen didn't answer. She couldn't find her voice. "It looks nice here. Is the fishing good?"

It was then she saw the fishing rod propped against a rock. This was more than she could stand. "Used to be," she spluttered. "It's polluted rotten now."

"Is it?" queried the surprised intruder. "It doesn't look like it."

In a few angry hops Aileen had skipped over the rocks until she was beside him. She pushed her face up into the boy's so that he could not mistake the meaning of her words,

"You're not looking where I'm looking, are you . . . Chookie Birdie?" she hissed. Then she pushed roughly past him almost tumbling him off his perch. Pure rage made her stop and shout back at the mortified boy, "Go away! Go on back to wherever you came from. This is my path, my hill, my beach!"

Robin Drake stood staring dumbly back at her.

"Are you deaf or something?" she screamed. "Go on! Clear off!"

She stood and watched until the boy moved away then she turned with an angry flourish and began to climb the steep path to the house.

Suddenly, a hoarse screech rent the air directly above her. Instinctively Aileen crouched down and raised her arms to cover her unprotected head. A whirlpool of flapping wings beat the air around her and then something stabbed her hand. The searing pain caused her to stumble and fall and as she fell she screamed out loud.

"Are you all right?"

Aileen had her eyes tightly shut and now she opened them warily. A dark figure was stooping over her. It took her a few seconds to recognise Hugh Bradley and when she did she ungratefully refused his helping hand and struggled to her feet by herself. Her breath came in loud gasps and her hands were shaking. A dark trickle of blood flowed from one. The hand was curled tightly round the little white figurine.

"They can be wicked when it's the lambing season," said Hugh. "I've known them to gouge out the eyes of a new-born when the ewe's back is turned. But there's no lambs now and I've never known them to attack people before."

The old man sounded puzzled and Aileen saw that he was staring at something behind her head. She turned and followed his gaze. At first she saw nothing and then a squawk drew her attention to a straggly tree that grew on the side of the hill. On the topmost branch, too thin it seemed to support its weight, perched a huge, hooded grey crow. The crow sat perfectly still and Aileen felt pierced through with the sharp glitter of its yellow eye.

"No," mused Hugh. "I've seen many things in my time but I've never seen the likes of that. Are you hurt bad?"

"It's only a scratch," she said quickly hiding the injured hand behind her back.

"Well, be sure and let Aggie Scroggy have a look at it. She's a wonder at the cures."

Aileen nodded dumbly. Secretly she decided that Aggie Scroggy was the last person on earth she would tell her business to. She ran on up the path and when she reached the top she looked back. Hugh Bradley was still standing staring after her.

She looked up at the house. It was a plain two-storeyed sensible dwelling standing on a natural shelf of level land tucked under the steep cliffs of Cloughderg Mountain. The mountain was crowned by a rounded crag of weather-beaten rock and on the flat step below the crag stood a long straight stone, pointing, like an accusing finger, at the sky. The peculiar outline made Cloughderg Mountain a landmark for miles around. For once Aileen was glad to see the house. As she passed the shed the door opened and Aggie Scroggy stepped out into her path carrying a basket of eggs. To avoid colliding with her, Aileen took a step backwards. The old woman turned and looked at her with a straight unblinking stare – a stare that searched for secrets.

"What happened your hand?" queried Aggie in her soft voice. The old woman was looking intently at Aileen's hand as if she knew exactly what lay hidden in the clenched fist. Aileen was sure that Aggie had witnessed the crow's attack from the darkness of the shed.

"Nothing. I scraped it on the rocks," muttered Aileen stuffing the hand and its hidden contents into her pocket. She looked away from the forget-me-not eyes and went indoors.

Her mother was working at some pots on the cooker.

"So there you are," she beamed pushing a strand of hair behind her ear. "I was going to send a search party after you. I suppose you were at the shore as usual?" A lump rose in Aileen's throat as she looked at her mother. She was so pretty with her glossy black curls and laughing grey eyes. Aileen loved her so much that it hurt.

"Umm," murmured Aileen.

"Umm! Is that all you have to say to your mother when she hasn't seen you all day?"

"Umm."

"It was lovely up in the field with Tom," murmured her mother dreamily. "I can't remember ever enjoying myself so much."

Aileen felt herself go cold and the pain of the last weeks grew worse.

"You should have come up."

"Why?" asked Aileen in her stiffest voice.

"What do you mean, 'why'?" asked her mother and her eyes grew clouded and troubled.

"You didn't need me – you had Tom Scroggy."

When Aileen had disappeared indoors Robin emerged from behind one of the large boulders that lay strewn over the hillside. He climbed the path slowly and stood silently beside Hugh Bradley.

The old man looked down and the puzzled frown vanished from his weather-beaten face. He smiled at Robin and put his arm around the thin shoulders.

"She gave you a right roasting didn't she, me boyo?" he chuckled. Robin hung his head and kicked aimlessly at a loose stone.

"She's horrible," he muttered. "I hate her!"

"It just came out of nowhere," the old man said and again he was looking at the big black and grey bird that still sat perched on the straggly tree. "Out of nowhere it came and straight into the attack. As if it knew exactly what it was doing."

"I hope it hurt her – real bad!" declared Robin with quiet vehemence.

"Shush now!" scolded Hugh as he gave the shoulders a comforting squeeze. "That's no way to be talking. I think Aileen is one very troubled wee lassie."

The worried look had returned to his face and he looked again at the tree and its evil occupant. The hooded crow glared balefully back at him then slowly it spread its powerful wings and sailed lazily away over the mountain.

"I hope she hasn't brought more bother on her head than she can cope with," Hugh mused almost to himself.

Coming abruptly out of his reverie, Hugh Bradley remembered the boy at his side who had troubles of his own.

"I was hoping you two could be friends," he said. "It would have been a bit of company for you out here."

"Friends!" gasped Robin. "She's as friendly as a Rottweiler! Just like the rest of them around here."

Hugh Bradley heard the bitterness in the words and sadly he turned and led the way to his home that nestled in a sheltered hollow on the other side of the hill.

"It isn't going to be easy for you here, son," he said when they were both settled round the big kitchen table, "but you have to give it time. Don't let them get you down. The Bradleys were never known to give in even when they were up against the worst that could be fired at them."

"Neither were the Drakes," said Robin.

"You're right there!" chuckled the old man ruefully and he was remembering a raw young man with a stubborn chin and a foreign accent who had sat at this same table and staked his claim on his daughter, his only child.

The door opened and the same daughter stood smiling fondly at the old man and the young boy.

"Ach, there you are yourself, Rosaleen," beamed Hugh. "Did you get your bits of business done?"

"Well, I got Robin into the school all right," said Rosaleen Drake as she took off her coat and joined them at the table. "Then I went into Derry and tramped around looking for a good dentist. The bus service is desperate! I was waiting nearly an hour before I got a bus that came all the way out to Cloughderg."

Rosaleen looked tired. She smiled at her son and said, "How did your first day go then?"

"Fine," said Robin without a blush. "They all seem very nice there."

His grandfather's approving wink made the lie worthwhile.

∽ Rows and Rumblings ∽

Back in the Scroggy kitchen Claire Kennedy, now Claire Scroggy, was feeling hurt and just a bit fed up with the sullen moods of her daughter.

"Aileen," she said with a note of determination in her voice, "your sulks have gone on long enough. I've just about had it with you, my girl. Sit down there. It's time we settled this once and for all."

How dare she! thought Aileen. How dare she blame me when it is all her fault.

She was too angry to answer and although she did sit down she moved to a low chair by the window to get as far away as possible. The chair was already occupied by the Scroggy cat but Aileen had no liking for cats so she dumped the sleek black-coated feline on to the floor. It glared at her resentfully before sliding out the door to chase the chickens.

Sighing, her mother lifted the chair Aileen had ignored and brought it over to the window. She sat facing her daughter.

"Come on now, love," she cajoled, "things can't go on like this. I spend most of my time making excuses for your behaviour. I'd hoped you'd eventually get back to normal but if anything you're getting worse. Trying to talk to you is like talking to a zombie. This time you're not leaving that chair until we have it out."

Aileen sat with her head lowered, her nervous fingers twirling a coil of fair hair. She said nothing but her brain was churning over a million questions that in the end boiled down to one – why did her mother have to go and spoil everything?

"Don't sit there talking to me in your head," snapped her mother. "If you have anything to say then say it straight out. I'm not putting up with you and your bad manners anymore. You only speak to Tom when you can't avoid it and you're downright rude to his mother."

Maybe it was the episode with the crow that spooked Aileen or maybe what was inside her was just bursting to get out. Suddenly she lost control of her temper and angry hurtful words came gushing out.

"They're all laughing at us," she blurted. "All of Drumenny and all of Cloughderg, and it's all because of you. We were all right the way we were. You had no need to go and get married again. And to marry the Scroggys – I mean, the Scroggys! Sure everybody knows they're not right in the head. She's as odd as two lefts and he's . . . he's an old man! How could you do it?"

"That's enough of that, Aileen!" snapped her mother.

"No, it's not," shouted Aileen. "You wanted me to talk and now I'm going to. You can't stop me just because you don't like what you're hearing." By this time she was crying with frustration. "Everything was great when there was just the two of us. Then you moved us out here without as much as asking me how I felt about it. I come home from school one day and you tell me you've got married again and I have to leave the town and my friends . . . and . . . and . . . what about my daddy? What do you think he'd have to say about you marrying into the Scroggys?"

And that, in Aileen's eyes, was exactly what had happened. Her happy life with a mother she adored had been cruelly torn away from her. They had lived right in the middle of the main street of Drumenny in a flat above Foley's the chemist where her mother worked. When Aileen came home from school she loved to help arrange all the lovely perfumes and scented soaps on the shelves. Her friends envied her when they saw her serving behind the counter and they thought her mother was gorgeous.

Aileen couldn't remember her father. He had died when she was only a few months old and he was not yet twenty-one. There was a photograph of him on a small table in the flat and Aileen loved that photograph. Her father, dressed in black studded leather, stood like a young god beside a glittering motor-bike. He was as fair as her mother was dark and it was from him that Aileen had inherited her blue eyes and long straight golden hair. His smile was cheeky and bursting with life and eighteen months after the photograph had been taken Paul Francis Kennedy was dead – killed on the motor-bike that had been his pride and joy.

The photograph had disappeared when they moved out to Cloughderg but Aileen searched through her mother's belongings until she found it and now it stood among her shore treasures on the little white wickerwork table beside her bed.

Claire Scroggy was deeply hurt by her daughter's words.

27

"Everything was not great above the chemist shop, Aileen," she said. "The flat was damp and I was out a fortune trying to heat it in the winter. I'm not qualified for anything and you don't get paid very much for selling worm powders and elastoplast. I was good at chatting up the farmers but all I was doing was parcelling up prescriptions. Charlie Foley paid me as much as he could, and he didn't bog his arm when it came to the rent for the flat, but making sure that you had everything your friends had wasn't easy and besides . . . I was very lonely."

"Lonely!" Aileen couldn't believe what she was hearing. "We were never lonely. There were people in and out of the shop all the time and we had plenty of friends . . . "

"*You* were never lonely, Aileen," interrupted her mother. "I was usually on my own when you were off gallivanting."

"You were not!" sobbed Aileen. "We had great times . . . you never said . . . "

"And then came Tom Scroggy," continued her mother as if she had never heard her. "Oh I know the Scroggys were thought a bit odd. But Tom came into the shop and he was quiet and gentle. And he's not an old man, Aileen, he's only twelve years older than me. We became friends and then we decided to get married. I didn't tell anyone in Drumenny because I knew what they would make of it around here. But I should have told you. I know that now and I'm heart sorry I didn't tell you. I was a coward. I didn't think you would understand . . . "

Claire stopped to take a breath and then she went on, "As for what your daddy would think . . . We were only children when we got married, Aileen. I loved Paul very much and when he died I thought I could never love anybody as much again. But I do Aileen. I love Tom Scroggy – in a different way from the way I loved your daddy – but every bit as much. I think Paul would approve of my choice."

Aileen didn't want to hear this. She put her hands over her ears and screamed, "But you didn't tell *me*!"

"It was a mistake not to tell you, Aileen, I admit it. Tom argued with me, he thought you should be told but I suppose . . . I suppose I was afraid you wouldn't take it well and I thought if everything happened very quickly and you were out here on Cloughderg Mountain in this nice house with the animals and the shore and everything . . . you would settle down. But I was wrong, wasn't I?"

"Yes you were wrong," blurted Aileen. "If you needed to marry again you could have married anybody you wanted – you're beautiful, you could have married anybody. But . . . but . . . Tom Scroggy and his daft mother! An old man and the Witch of Cloughderg! When I was small I used to run after her in the town to see if I could catch her casting a spell. *Everybody* says she's crazy. She talks to the fairies! Oh you were wrong all right!"

Claire Scroggy was by now very angry and very agitated. She moved away from her daughter in case she was tempted to reach out and strike her. She got out of the chair and moved over to the cooker where she steadied herself on the chrome bar used for drying tea-cloths. She kept her back to Aileen not trusting herself to face the sobbing child.

"Let there be no misunderstanding, Aileen," she said

in a low controlled voice. "I did *not* mean that I was wrong to marry Tom. The mistake I made was not telling you. I had hoped you'd be a bit more grown-up about this but you're behaving like a baby – a very spoilt, selfish baby."

Aileen attempted to interrupt but her mother silenced her and went on.

"Tom and his mother have both made you very welcome here. It has meant a big change for them too. They're not used to children and Aggie could have been very difficult if she wanted. She's had Tom to herself since his father died thirty years ago and she has never had to share her kitchen with another woman. Instead she's been like a mother to me and she would be a granny to you if you'd let her."

"I don't need a granny, not a queer one anyway." The last sentence was spoken with as much sarcasm as Aileen could get into her voice.

"Stop it, Aileen," shouted her mother, "stop that nonsense at once!"

At that moment the back door opened and Tom Scroggy came in. He could see immediately that something was badly wrong.

"Are you all right, Claire?" he enquired. "What are you getting yourself upset about now?" His eyes went from mother to child in uneasy concern. He moved over to his wife and put his arm round her. She laid her head on his broad shoulder.

Aileen slipped away into her own room. She felt more left out than she had ever felt before.

Once in her room she went straight to the photograph of her father and looked at it for a long time. Then she took the little statue from her pocket and placed it beside the photograph and next to the foreign boxes, the clouded glass and the twisted driftwood. As she left the room she looked at the statue and the serene face smiled back at her.

At the dinner table that night Aileen was her usual silent self but she listened. For a change there was something to listen to.

"I see Rosaleen Bradley's back home," said Tom to his wife.

"Rosaleen? Is she indeed?" queried Claire and Aileen could see that her mother was pleased at the news.

"Aye," continued Tom. "I was talking to her up in the field there just after you left. She came home on Saturday."

"And has she the boy with her?"

"She has that," answered Tom, "and he's at the school already."

"Poor Rosaleen," replied her mother. "She hasn't had it easy either. And the coming home will be hard – especially for the boy. I must call down and see her. We were at school together you know. We were the best of friends Rosaleen and I . . . " Claire Scroggy's face lit up as she told tales of their childish pranks.

Aileen realised that the boy they were talking about had to be Robin Drake and Rosaleen Bradley was his mother but who and where was his father? And why was it 'hard' for them to come back to Cloughderg? Aileen was dying to ask questions but she couldn't because that would mean she would have to join in the conversation. She bit her tongue and swallowed her curiosity, pretending to be totally disinterested. Then she saw that Aggie Scroggy was watching her. That old woman always seemed to be watching her.

When dinner was over and the dishes washed Aileen escaped once again to her room and pretended to do a bit of homework. Though she wouldn't for the world admit it to anyone, she loved this room. The walls were whitewashed and the duvet on the bed was a riot of mad colours. She had her table and a small desk and chair. It had a wooden floor with a rug for comfort and that was just the way Aileen wanted it. Her mother thought the room was very bare and would have filled it with patchwork cushions and frilly drapes if Aileen had allowed her. The room wasn't sparse at all; it was full of her jeans and shorts and T-shirts, baseball boots and runners and a scattering of books.

The walls of the old house were thick and the window-sill was deep enough to curl up on. This was Aileen's favourite perch. Once she pulled the heavy curtains, she was shut off from the world. From there, high up under the eaves of the house, Aileen could see down to the shore and away out over the waters to the far side of Lough Foyle. Tonight a new moon swung cheekily in the indigo sky and near it shone the evening star, casting its sheen on the calm waters. Aileen sat without a light so that the scenery would not be dimmed by the harsh glare of electricity. She sat trying to sort out everything that had happened to her that day but she was too tired and soon she pulled back the curtains, slid off the window-sill and under the duvet.

Tired as she was Aileen did not have a peaceful night. She dreamed strange dreams in which she was pursued relentlessly by a black shapeless shadow. She woke with a start and her body was bathed in sweat. It was still dark outside and the morning rooster had not yet crowed his importance to the sun. Through her window, a single shaft of light from the young moon cast a steely glow on the little statue on her table. The ugly face grimaced menacingly at her. Aileen was absolutely sure that when she had placed the statue on the table she had turned the ugly face towards the wall!

∾ A Mystery and a Butterfly ∾

To his relief there was no one at the bus stop the next morning when Robin arrived there punctually at 8:30 a.m. He hadn't been looking forward to meeting Aileen again and had no great wish to be alone with her for any length of time. She came panting up the lane just as the bus came into sight. They boarded the empty bus and sat on opposite sides. Robin stared intently out the window. Once he glanced furtively in Aileen's direction and caught her looking at him – not with the anger she had displayed on the beach but with open curiosity.

As the other children were picked up in twos and threes they went into whispering huddles and an excited buzz filled the bus. There was a lot of nudging and giggling and all the interest was concentrated on Robin Drake. A very interesting piece of gossip was flowing round the bus like an electric current. Aileen realised that every child knew something about the boy that she didn't. Robin was very aware that he was the subject of all the gossip and he began to sink into a state of despair.

Battler and Co piled on to the bus in a raucous heap of flying arms and boots. They seemed to know the sensational news already and had even more titbits to add. The noise from the back of the bus abated slightly to a more orderly whispering that hinted at the hatching of a plan. Then there was an ominous silence.

The silence didn't last too long. From the back of the bus came a parade led by Battler Doherty. Himself, Wee Willie Clements and Ronan McCafferty marched down the aisle as smartly as the swaying of the bus allowed.

"ATTEN . . . SHUN!" barked the Battler when they reached Robin Drake and his comrades stiffened to attention and made exaggerated salutes.

"All PRESENT AND CORRECT, S-A-A-A-RN MAJOR!" screeched Wee Willie.

"HAA . . . BOUT . . . TTT . . . URNN!" And the parade started again down to the back of the bus and all the other children in the bus chanted, "LEFT, RIGHT – LEFT, RIGHT!" and clapped in marching rhythm until Fonsie McKee, the bus driver, got fed up and roared, "If yous crowd of hooligans don't sit down and have a bit of manners I'll have the lot of yez into Lambeg and I hope he roasts the aaa . . . uh . . . behinds . . . off yez!"

Even Mrs McCloskey was different with the new pupil. She too knew something that Aileen didn't. Robin Drake was no longer a botheration, a stray wasp that had flown into the room with the sole intention of annoying the teacher. Instead he was given the full "Mrs Mac Special". This was worse than being treated as a nuisance. Mrs McCloskey was doing what she liked doing best – being nice to special cases.

"What do *you* think about that, Robin?" she would say. Or, "What lovely writing! You're a credit to the teachers who taught you, Robin Drake," and, "Will you all look at this, children. If I could get half as good out of you lot I could retire in peace!"

Robin knew the teacher was trying to make him feel

at home but he wished she would stop. All this special attention was only making him more of a target.

Although it was October the weather was still warm and lunch-time was spent on the playground. This was a scraped out cinder-covered patch at the back of the school. A low stone wall separated the playground from cultivated fields full of potato tops and turnip heads. Aileen liked the fine weather. She could hunch herself up on the wall, eat her sandwiches, look at the potatoes and mind her own business – if she was allowed to. Today she was allowed to because all the attention was on Robin Drake. He too had tried to find himself a private place further along the wall but he was not to be left in peace.

Battler Doherty and his adjutants gathered the whole class into marching formation in front of Robin and some of the wee ones rushed to join in the fun although, like Aileen, they hadn't the least idea what it was all about. Up and down they marched in parade ground fashion while Battler barked the orders. Lisa McCarron and Nuala Deery had made drums out of their lunch boxes and were banging them to the thumping beat of the marching feet.

Ronan McCafferty was particularly vicious; he did a lot of prodding at Robin Drake and he was taunting him unmercifully but Aileen couldn't hear what he was saying. Robin sat with his back turned to the teasing, looking at the field and Aileen knew how he felt for that was how she usually spent her lunch-times.

By now Ronan was very annoyed because Robin Drake continued to ignore him and he began to shout at the top of his voice. This time Aileen could hear him.

"We don't want no rotten Brits here!" he shouted.

Then he began to chant "BRITS OUT! BRITS OUT!" The others took up the refrain as they continued marching.

"BRITS OUT! BRITS OUT!"

The school bell clanged loudly from the doorway. Robin's torture was over but he knew that it was just for the moment. With all his heart he wished his mother had never come back to Ireland.

By the end of the day Aileen was no wiser about the mystery that surrounded Robin Drake and when the bus stopped at the lane she was tempted to talk to him to see what she could find out. But she just couldn't bring herself to do it.

Rogue, the Scroggy Border Collie, came lolloping to meet her when she pushed open the gate to the farmyard. Scattering chickens in his wake he brought a smile to Aileen's face as he twisted himself in contortions of delight at seeing her. She ran indoors to throw her schoolbag in her bedroom and Rogue waited patiently at the door hoping they would soon be heading to the shore.

But today, Aileen didn't head to the shore, much to Rogue's disappointment. Instead she found herself lurking around the Bradley house hoping to get some clue about the mystery of Robin Drake. The house was quiet. She sat in her spying place for over half an hour. Once a young woman, with sandy hair scraped back in a pony tail, came out and threw some scraps to the hens and then Hugh Bradley and Robin Drake went to the ramshackle shed where Hugh did all his tinkering. From the clanging and banging she heard she guessed they wouldn't be coming out for a long time. So she went wandering on down the lane. As she passed the overgrown narrow path that led to the derelict fishermen's cottages she noticed that the grass had been flattened by the wheels of a car. This was most peculiar. Driven by curiosity, she walked down the path and as she reached the cottages she saw a most surprising sight.

A small loaf-shaped car was parked outside the door of the middle cottage. It was no ordinary car. For a start, it was most peculiarly coloured. The car was white but it was decorated with a huge yellow daisy and bright green leaves. The name 'Daisy' was boldly emblazoned across the bonnet in decorative black print.

The boot of the car was open and a mountain of technicolor cushions, towels and blankets was moving towards the door of the cottage. Spellbound, Aileen watched as the mountain tilted sideways and slid to the ground scattering debris everywhere.

"Blast! And blast again!" An exasperated apparition struggled vainly to recapture her escaped belongings. It was a girl, nearly a woman, and she was some sight! She wore a luminous pink and green striped top that swung loosely over a pair of legs clad in glaring orange leggings. The legs were long and shapely and the feet encased in rigidly laced ox-blood Doc Marten boots – boots that Aileen would have died for!

"What are you standing there gawping for?" called the girl. "Come and give me a hand."

Aileen darted forward delighted to be of service to such an exotic creature but Rogue took off home like a bullet. Without noticing the dog's reaction, she gathered fat cushions and all the errant bric-à-brac scattered on the ground.

"Just dump it anywhere inside the door," said the girl and Aileen found herself looking into a grinning face topped by a wild crop of spiked white hair. Two enormous earrings dangled from a pair of dainty ears and purple-black lipstick defined the generously full lips. A pair of grey eyes glinted from a graveyard of black eyeliner and smudged mascara. She looked like a tropical butterfly that had been blown off course.

"I'm Vale Prentess," said the girl as she off-loaded a tangled heap of fringes, fans and furbelows in the middle of the less than clean floor, "and am I glad to see you! What's your name?"

"Aileen," said Aileen. "Aileen Kennedy."

"Well, Aileen Kennedy," said Vale Prentess, "what are you doing in this god-forsaken part of the world?"

"I live here," muttered Aileen dying to ask the same question of the girl.

"Well, I suppose somebody has to," beamed Vale and she looked around the chaos that surrounded her. "It looks like a bomb-site, doesn't it?"

"Are you really going to live here?" asked Aileen incredulously.

Vale threw back her shining blonde head and laughed a hearty laugh. "Don't be so shocked. I've lived in worse. I'll only be here for a couple of months at the most."

"All by yourself?"

"Of course. I'm a big girl now! I've finished my degree and I am working for a master's."

Aileen was stunned. The girl didn't look very bookish. "What does that mean?" she asked.

"It means I have to write a big, long, boring essay called a dissertation and that is why I am out here. I'm going round lots of isolated places collecting stories and all sorts of memories from the old people. I'm trying to gather old legends and customs and superstitions. Cloughderg is supposed to be full of them."

"Well, Aggie Scroggy is full of them anyway," mumbled Aileen.

"Who's Aggie Scroggy?"

"She's a daft old woman."

"Well, there you are. I've made a start already. Perhaps you can be my assistant? I could do with all the help I can get."

There was nothing Aileen would have liked better than to be assistant to Vale Prentess. She could just see the faces of the people in Cloughderg and Drumenny when they feasted their eyes on this visitor.

"We'll talk about that another time," decided the girl. "Help me now to bring a bit of organisation to this place."

An hour later a fire had been lit in the abandoned fireplace and a big fluffy sleeping bag was stretched out beside it surrounded by a bank of cushions. Books were piled neatly against a crumbling wall, a box of groceries stored well away from the heat of the fire and a kettle was boiling furiously on a small primus stove.

"There now," said Vale, "all the comforts of a first class hotel. I'm glad the pump in the yard is still working. Will you join me in a cup of tea and drink a toast to my first night in Cloughderg?"

She lit the forest of candles that she had stacked on the window-sill, put on a tape of music that was all tinkling bells and soft guitars and then placed two smoking dishes on the floor one each side of the fireplace. A sweet pungent smell filled the air.

"That's incense," she informed Aileen. "It adds a

touch of the mysterious, doesn't it? Come and sit beside me." And she plonked herself down on a pile of plump cushions.

Aileen spent another hour in the cottage and didn't even notice the time passing. Vale entertained her with outrageous stories about her student escapades and then allowed her to poke through her belongings – a great tumbling of feather boas, beads and twisted silken skeins of whisper-soft fabric.

"That's an Indian sari," said Vale when she saw that Aileen was particularly interested in a flimsy swathe of crimson and gold. "Would you like to try it on?"

"Could I?" asked Aileen breathlessly.

"'Course you can but you'd better slip off that sweatshirt. You won't get the proper effect over that." Aileen had a T-shirt on underneath so she quickly pulled off her sweatshirt.

Vale began to cocoon her in the diaphanous silk until there was just enough of the roll left to drape over her shoulder and loop over her arm.

"Oh, it's gorgeous," whispered Aileen. "I wish I could see myself."

"You look lovely," said Vale. But something about the girl's voice had changed and Aileen looked up at her. She was no longer smiling and there was a displeased look in her eyes.

"I'm a bit tired now, Aileen," she said. "I've had a long day so if you don't mind I'd like to rest for a while."

Aileen was a little disappointed. She would have liked to have stayed another while in the cottage with Vale. As she made her way home her spirits lifted. She had found somebody she could talk to. Somebody young and exciting. Maybe life wasn't so bad after all. She gave Rogue a special hug when he came to meet her to make up for not taking him to the shore.

Remembering that she was still in her mother's bad books, she hurried in case she would be late for the evening meal and so bring more trouble on herself. The kitchen was empty and the pots were still burbling merrily on the big yellow cooker. She had plenty of time so she decided to go to her room and listen to some tapes.

On the landing outside her bedroom she met Aggie Scroggy. The old woman seemed to be a bit flustered. "The dinner's nearly ready, Aileen," she said.

"I'll be down in a minute," said Aileen. As soon as she entered her room, Aileen knew that someone had been in there. And she knew who that someone was. There was a smell of cinnamon lozenges in the air. Aggie Scroggy had no business being in her room. She had never crossed the door – until today. What had taken her in now?

Aileen looked around. Everything appeared to be as it should be. Then she looked at her sea collection. Something was slightly out of place there. The little white statue was leaning drunkenly against the driftwood as if someone had replaced it in a hurry. So this was what Aggie was interested in! Aileen picked up the two-faced trinket and as she stared at it she became convinced that if she hadn't returned at that precise moment she never would have seen it again.

Clearly Aggie Scroggy would steal the statue the moment she had the opportunity. Why? Aileen asked herself. What did she want with it? It was a mystery. Whatever it was all about Aileen knew that her beach find had an importance that she had yet to discover. From now on she would never be without it. She went to her cupboard and took a lace from one of her battered runners and strung it through the hole at the top of the statue. Then she tied the lace around her neck. The figurine was hers – a gift from the sea, and no one was going to touch it again.

∽ Surprise! Surprise! ∽

For the second night running Aileen's sleep was disturbed. Dreams tumbled through her mind in a confusion of ever-changing images. In the morning, feeling exhausted and on edge, she went into the kitchen for breakfast. Tom Scroggy had just finished a bowl of porridge and was about to leave the house.

"Good morning, Aileen," he said. "It's grand weather for the time of year."

"Morning," mumbled Aileen and then seeing her mother's warning look, she strained to smile and added, "Yes it is nice isn't it?"

Aileen knew her mother was right about Tom but she wouldn't admit it openly. He was a kind man and she felt a stab of guilt when she saw how her pleasant words and smile pleased him. Claire placed a mountain of toast at the table and glanced approvingly at her daughter.

"Eat up, pet," she said, "or you'll be galloping after the bus as usual."

Aggie Scroggy came in from the yard carrying a clutch of freshly laid eggs. Her coal black cat was at her heels. The sleek animal came as far as the threshold of the door and then shrank back and stood rigid, like a frozen frame in a moving film. Her back arched and her fur stiffened.

44

"What's up with her?" laughed Tom. "You'd think she'd seen a pack of greyhounds."

The cat was staring at Aileen and the slitted gaze made her feel even more on edge. Why was the thing looking at her like that?

"Shoo!" urged Aggie and the cat scampered back out to the yard to disappear under a bucket. It's something to do with her, Aileen decided, I bet she has the poor animal terrified of me.

Out in the yard, Tom was revving up his ancient tractor in preparation for the day's work. Rogue was leaping about biting at the tyres anxious to be off to the fields.

"Rogue," Aileen called wanting to give the dog his usual cuddle before leaving for school. But Rogue did not come bouncing in his giddy boisterous fashion. Instead he tucked his tail between his legs, whined as if a bee had stung his tender nose, and slunk away behind the tractor.

Hurt and puzzled, Aileen left him in his refuge and went on to get her bus. What was wrong with her today? Had Aggie the power to turn the animals against her so that she hadn't a friend left in the world?

School that day was very busy. It was the last school day before the mid-term break and the Drumenny Community Centre was having its annual Halloween festival on the following Saturday night. The pupils had to make most of the decorations. The younger children were making bats and cats but the top class were working on a large witch to hang from the ceiling.

By the middle of the afternoon the finishing touches

had been put to the masterpiece and Mrs McCloskey asked Aileen, Robin and Battler Doherty to carry it to the storeroom to await collection. Their route lay across the playground and down a grassy slope to the small shed that housed extra desks and tattered books. When they were in the storeroom and out of hearing range, Battler began to howl the theme from an old Robin Hood television programme – but he had his own set of words:

Robin Drake, Robin Drake
What a poncy name.
Robin Drake, Robin Drake,
We know why he came.
His Da's done a bunk
And his Ma got a gonk,
Robin Drake, Robin Drake, Robin Drake.

Aileen sensed a fierce tension in the boy beside her, a tension that he had never displayed before, no matter how vicious the teasing had been. Battler sensed it too. He had broken through Robin Drake's self-protective outer skin and now he was going in for the kill. Robin walked quickly out of the room and climbed the grassy slope.

"Hey, did your Ma finally find out what the Brits are like then?" Battler shouted at the stiff back of the boy. Then he climbed up after him. "Your oul' woman's nothing but a rotten army cast-off," he said prodding Robin with a thick finger.

Aileen was still standing paralysed at the bottom of the slope. She knew that something awful was going to happen. Robin Drake faced up to his very large tormentor; his face was composed but deathly pale. "You will take that back and apologise," he said in a calm, controlled voice.

"Oh yeh?" wheezed Battler. "And what if I don't?"

"Then I will make you," said Robin.

Aileen couldn't believe her ears. Either Robin Drake was very stupid or very brave, or both. If he raised a fist to Battler Doherty he would be flattened in seconds. Battler seemed to swell and grow purple with indignation.

"You're a cheeky wee ball of snot, aren't you?" he sneered.

"And you are a thick, ignorant brute," replied Robin. "I will give you one more chance – apologise for what you said."

Aileen's mouth dropped open in amazement. Battler too was dumbfounded for a second, then he burst out laughing.

"You've a big mouth for a wee squirt, haven't you? We'll see how big it is with no teeth." And the hulking bruiser took a swing at the small chalk-white face. The swing was so powerful that Battler almost knocked himself off his feet. Robin gave a slight flick of his head and the bunched fist sailed past him.

The surprise had hardly registered on Battler's puffy features before Robin moved swiftly towards him and suddenly he was hoisted clean off the ground. He hovered for a second in mid-air and then came flying down the slope to land at Aileen's feet in a heap of flailing arms and legs.

"Apologise for what you said about my mother," demanded Robin from his superior height. Battler muttered something unintelligible and his assailant leaped down the slope and stood over him. "I didn't hear you," he said mildly.

"All right, all right," said a green-faced Battler. "I shouldn't have said nothin' about her."

"And my father?"

"Yeh, he's OK too," sniffled Battler.

Satisfied, Robin quickly scaled the slope and set off across the playground with his hands in his pockets.

It took Aileen a while to recover but when she did she went haring off after Robin.

"Hey, wait!" she called. Robin slowed down and waited for her. "How did you do that?"

"What?"

"That," she pointed over her head in the direction of Battler. "How did you throw that great lump of raw beef over your shoulder as if he was a . . . a . . . an empty bag?"

"That's just what he is."

Robin hadn't answered her question and she didn't like to ask it again.

"Karate," said Robin at last. "My dad's a black belt. I have been learning it as long as I can remember."

"You mean you could do that all the time and you just sat there in the playground and let them chew you up?"

Robin shrugged and walked on silently.

"Why?" asked Aileen.

"Because then they were only getting at me," replied Robin. "He shouldn't have said those things about my mum and dad."

"But nobody saw it happen!" protested Aileen. "And if I tell anybody you threw Battler Doherty over your shoulder they'll laugh at me. You'll have to do it again when everybody's there."

"No way!" smiled Robin. "I don't want them queuing up to have a go at me."

A sudden shyness came over Aileen when she realised that she was talking to Robin Drake. She blushed with shame when she remembered the last words she had spoken to him.

"The things Battler was saying – they were rotten," she volunteered by way of apology.

"Do you think they were true?"

"I dunno," said Aileen. "All I know about you is that your mother was Rosaleen Bradley and she went to live in England."

"Well you must be the only one around here who hasn't been talking about us." Robin seemed to struggle with his thoughts for a moment, then he came to a decision. "My mother married a British soldier. He was stationed in Derry during a tour of duty and the two of them had to leave and go to England. But my dad didn't walk out on us. He was spending a lot of time overseas and my mum got more and more homesick. They decided to separate, that's all. I'll be going over most holidays to see him and he writes every week."

"Have you been overseas too?" asked Aileen.

"I've been loads of places but mostly Germany."

"Do you miss him – your dad?"

Robin nodded and for a while he couldn't speak. Aileen felt every pain he was feeling. "Yeh, he's great, my dad. We go camping and fishing and do all sorts of things together."

"Couldn't you have stayed with him?"

"No – army regulations and all that. Besides, I couldn't let my mum come home on her own."

For the first time in many weeks the thought occurred to Aileen that she wasn't the only one in the world who was miserable.

Just as they reached the classroom door a hand grabbed her and she was hauled back into the corridor. Battler Doherty pushed her up against the wall and pressed his face close to hers. "If you breathe a word of what happened out there," he said in a violent whisper, "you'll wish you'd never been born."

When Aileen got on the bus that afternoon she saw Battler slumped against a window pretending to be asleep. The gang were trying to coax a bit of life into him but he just grunted at them irritably and they gave up. Robin Drake was sitting by himself in his usual seat near the front. Aileen drew a deep breath and then went to sit beside him. There was a great whoop of delight from Lisa McCarron.

"Look at the two love-birds!" she crowed. "Go on, Aileen, give your new boyfriend a big smackerooo." A chorus of wolf-whistles accompanied by loud smacking noises filled the bus.

"I think maybe you should give me a few karate lessons," smiled Aileen and Robin smiled back.

They walked together down the lane chattering like old friends and by the time they said goodbye they had arranged to meet the next day which was a Friday, the first day of their holiday. When Aileen turned the corner of the lane and the gate to the Scroggy farm came into view all thoughts of Robin Drake left her head. Aggie Scroggy was standing there and she was talking to Vale Prentess! The girl had recording equipment strung over her shoulder and she was waving her hands about. They seemed to be having a row. Aggie lifted her thin arm and pointed down the lane. She was ordering Vale to leave!

Aileen waited for Vale to reach her, hoping to find out what the trouble was but the girl just brushed angrily past her.

"You're right," she almost spat. "She is an old bag."

Aggie was still standing at the gate when Aileen spoke to her. "What's up? Why did you chase her away?"

"I don't like that young woman and I don't want her snooping about the house."

"Why? Just because she dresses funny? She's only collecting old stories for her desert . . . for her essay."

"Yes, so she tells me. I don't trust her and I think you would be wise not to be in her company, Aileen."

"She's my friend, and I'll be in her company if I want to," answered Aileen hotly.

"You must choose your own friends, of course," answered Aggie, "but you should learn to choose wisely."

The bubble of anger that always seemed to be on the boil inside Aileen erupted. She whirled round and went in search of Vale. She found her in her cottage and the girl's temper was almost a match for Aileen's.

"I only wanted to ask her a few questions," she shouted as she hurled cushions around the room. "To get her to tell me some of the stories she remembers from her childhood but the old witch ordered me off. I don't know how you live with her, Aileen."

Vale's anger evaporated rapidly and soon the pair were sipping tea and talking nineteen to the dozen. Vale related some more of her adventures as she sailed around the countryside in "Daisy" and she giggled as she described the shocked faces of the farmers when they saw her spiked hair, frayed jeans and Doc Martens. Not to be outdone, Aileen described the look on Battler Doherty's face as he was launched into space over Robin Drake's shoulder.

"You should have seen him," she giggled weeping with laughter. "One minute he was scowling like a man-eating tiger and the next he was blubbering like a baby."

They laughed together for a while and then Vale reached into a folder and drew something out. "Talking about different faces," she said, "I wonder if you have seen anything like this around?" She placed some drawings on Aileen's knee. They were all of stones with two faces.

"I'm hoping to come across something like this while I'm here. They are called Janus Stones and several good examples have been found in this area. They date way back to pre-Christian times. It would be terrific if I could find one. It would give a great boost to my work."

Aileen stared at the drawings. The huge stones looked clumsy and crude and although they did have two faces they weren't a bit like her tiny statue.

"Have you seen anything like that, Aileen?" asked Vale.

"No."

"Nothing at all?"

Aileen shook her head but her hand wandered instinctively to the neck of her sweatshirt.

"Well if you do," smiled Vale taking back the drawings, "be sure and let me know."

As she made her way home Aileen wondered why she hadn't told Vale about the statue. It's not what she's looking for, she decided, it doesn't look a bit like those drawings.

Again when Aileen entered the yard, the cat vanished under a gap in the door of the barn and Rogue slid away to cower under a trailer. Even the hens seemed to cluck warily and scuttle away. She ignored them and cursed Aggie Scroggy.

Dinner was not yet ready so she went to throw her bag in her room as she had no homework to do over the holiday. She stopped at her door and drew a sharp breath. Someone had been in her room again and this time the intruder was less careful than before. The drawers of her dressing table were half open and underwear was trailing out of them. Her wardrobe had been thoroughly searched and even the quilt on her bed was topsy-turvey.

Aggie Scroggy again! she thought grimly. I disturbed her the last time and now she has come back again and when the statue wasn't on the table she ransacked the place looking for it.

Aileen pulled the little statue out from under her T-shirt and examined it. Why was Aggie so interested in it? It couldn't be worth any money and anyway Aggie wasn't the type to be interested in money. Aileen made up her mind. The statue was hers – given to her by the sea – and if there was a mystery about it then she was the one who was going to solve it.

Suddenly she raised her head and sniffed. There was a faint familiar odour in the air. She sniffed again. She knew that smell but she couldn't place it. It was not the smell of cinnamon lozenges.

∾ A Dreadful Meeting ∾

Robin pulled across the bar of the gate that led to Scroggy's yard. It seemed empty and he hoped he hadn't come too early. A soft voice surprised him.

"You must be Robin. I was wondering when I would meet you."

A small figure, a neat little old woman, was carrying two buckets almost full of milk. He reached for one of the buckets and said, "Let me help you."

So this was Aggie Scroggy. His grandfather had told him the story behind Aileen Kennedy and the Scroggys but he was still a bit confused. Hugh Bradley thought Aggie was the cream on top of the milk but he sensed that Aileen had a different opinion.

"I'm looking for Aileen," he said.

"She's around somewhere," smiled Aggie, "and while you're waiting, you can help me feed the calves."

The byre they entered was low roofed and very dark. The air was warm and heavy with body smells that came as a shock to a town nose used to chimney smoke and exhaust fumes. As Robin grew accustomed to the darkness he could distinguish dark shapes and the whites of eyes. Three wobbly calves, sensing that feeding time had arrived, strained at the wooden slats of their manger and mooed softly.

"You have to put your hand into the milk," instructed Aggie, "and let them suck your fingers. They think they are feeding from their mothers."

Robin was horrified. He hesitated.

"Go on. Put your hand in."

He plunged his hand into the warm creamy fluid, balanced the bucket on a wooden slat and tucked it under the chin of a black and white calf. The calf dipped his nose in the bucket and then found the fingers. Robin's hand was trapped between the strong jaws. He felt the rasping of the tongue as it investigated his trembling fingers and then the sucking began. It was strong and urgent. He could feel the rough-ridged roof of the calf's mouth and his fingers were almost pulled from their sockets. But he wasn't tempted to remove them. As it fed the calf gazed up at him and Robin felt wonderful. He laughed a nervous laugh.

"Rub his head with your other hand, round about where his horns will grow," said Aggie, and Robin could see her smile at his pleasure. He rubbed the head and the sucking grew less nervous and steadied to a calm contented rhythm.

"I'm glad to see you and Aileen getting to know each other," mused Aggie. "I think she needs a good friend. Her world is upside down now and she'll have a long hard struggle to get comfortable in it."

"I know how she feels."

"Yes, you do in a way. But you are different, you two. Aileen lives in a world of dreams and maybes but I think your feet know where they are. I'm going to tell you something, Robin, because I think I should. I believe that Aileen has been drawn into a world that she doesn't understand – a world that could be very dangerous. At the minute she has trust in nobody but she will need to trust somebody and it needs to be somebody who is a true friend."

Robin didn't know what to say in reply so he said nothing. The calf's tongue was now scraping against the bottom of the empty bucket but it would not release his fingers. He took the bucket away and still the calf sucked greedily at his trapped hand.

"He's full up," laughed Aggie. "He's just looking for comfort now."

When Robin emerged from the darkness of the byre into the daylight he saw Aileen standing by the gate looking a bit lost. She was surprised when she saw him.

"I was waiting for you," she said accusingly. "I thought you weren't coming.'

"Aggie asked me to help feed the calves."

"She would. If she thought you were looking for me she would send you the top of Cloughderg Mountain on a message."

Feeding the calves was usually Aileen's job and it was one she enjoyed. But today she had been sent to cut nettles for the young turkeys. She knew that she was just being kept out of the way because everybody had noticed that she was unsettling the animals.

"Why don't you like her?" asked Robin. "I thought she was nice. And she's worried about you."

"She is my hat," snapped Aileen. "I just want her to keep her nose out of my business, that's all. Come on, I want to get as far away as possible from this place."

"Aileen," called Claire Scroggy from the door of the house, "when you're passing Bradleys' call and ask Robin's mum and his grandfather to come over for tea tonight. You're invited too of course," she smiled at Robin.

Robin would have been blind and deaf if he hadn't noticed the effect Aileen had on the animals around the yard. The hens clucked worriedly as she passed and hurried to be clear of her. The dog cowered with his body stretched flat, his head resting on his outstretched paws and his watchful eyes following her progress. Even the cows refused to come out of the milking byre until Aileen had closed the gate of the yard behind her. Tom Scroggy scolded the cows and scratched his head in puzzlement.

"Did you see that?" demanded Aileen when they were well down the lane. "She has set everything against me."

"You can't be blaming Aggie because the cows are taking peculiar notions?"

"So," replied Aileen, "she has you on her side too, has she?"

This business of taking sides in something he didn't understand didn't rest easy with Robin. After they had delivered the invitation, they wandered on down the lane.

"There's one ugly customer who isn't flying away from you," said Robin pointing towards the hedge. A hooded crow was sitting there quietly watching them. Aileen was sure it was the same crow that had attacked her a few days ago.

"Scram," she shouted. "Clear off you mangy bag of feathers!"

The bird did fly off. But not very far. It came to rest again on a rock in the open hillside. Aileen found a gap in the hedge and began to walk towards the rock.

"Where are you going?" asked Robin.

"Dunno," replied Aileen. "It's up to something. I want to find out what."

The grey crow moved quietly on again and sat waiting for Aileen to get almost within reach before flying off to rest on another rock.

"It almost seems as if it is telling us to follow," said Robin hesitantly. Aileen didn't answer but continued to be lured on by the winged coaxer. They were now well out of sight of any habitation and were picking their steps carefully through true wilderness. Behind them Cloughderg Mountain pointed its stony finger and in front of them they could see the mound of Grianan Hill and the ancient stone fort at the summit.

"I don't know if this is a good idea," said Robin. "I don't know my way about the hills and I don't think you do either."

"Don't be daft," said Aileen. "We can't get lost. And have you anything better to do? We'll just go on another bit."

Reluctantly, Robin followed and as they went deeper into the wilds, he began to experience a thrill of fear. There was something about Aileen Kennedy that made him feel the presence of danger and excitement. The bird flew on and then suddenly disappeared behind a rugged outcrop of rocks that blocked their path and view ahead. Aileen increased her speed and instinctively Robin raced after her. A dreadful premonition urged him on. Just as Aileen reached the rock he grabbed her jacket and pulled her back.

"What are you doing," she protested struggling. "Let me go!" Then she stopped struggling and her breath hissed through her teeth. They were standing on the edge of a sheer cliff! One more step and Aileen would have gone plunging down to meet the spiked rocks that littered the floor of the narrow valley.

It wasn't really a valley; nothing as natural as a river had carved that vicious crack in the hillside. It was a harsh, barren place, totally isolated from the rest of the world. Nothing grew there and nothing seemed to live there. The air was choked with silence. Not a bird sang and not an insect buzzed.

Across the deep gash the crow sat waiting on a narrow ledge. As they watched, the outline of the bird began to change. It wobbled and blurred and grew and then the image cleared. In the place of the crow stood a tall woman. She was dressed in a robe of wispy grey that was clasped at the waist by a belt of glittering jet beads. About her shoulders was draped a luxurious black cloak that flowed with the lines of her body. The cloak was fastened at a pale throat with a hooked bird claw. The talons of the claw shone darkly with the rich gleam of precious jewels.

The woman was beautiful but her beauty was cold and terrible. Her face was ivory pale and her ebony hair fell around her shoulders like a polished helmet. Her head was encircled with a writhing snake wrought in gold. The head of the reptile reared up above the white forehead and the eyes had the icy glitter of diamonds; the tongue was a fiery river of rubies. In one white hand the woman held a thin rod and at the end of the rod the snake-head reared again.

As Robin and Aileen stood transfixed the woman spoke and her voice was soft and alluring.

"Do not be afraid. I am your friend. Come with me now and you shall have your heart's desire."

The cloying sweetness of the voice enthralled Aileen and she wanted to go with this woman even into the dark foreboding valley. The deep slit that separated them was so narrow that when the woman extended her hand Aileen felt she could reach out and touch it.

"Come," coaxed the woman. "Come and I will show you visions never before seen by the human eye."

Robin too felt the draw of the hypnotic voice but he also sensed that he was not included in the invitation. There was a movement by his side and he saw Aileen step out into mid-air. Slowly she began to descend into the abyss. She sailed smoothly as if riding on an invisible escalator. The woman kept pace with her and together they dropped effortlessly into the deepening gloom. Aileen was mesmerised by the woman's eyes. They were large and very beautiful and, in the half shadows, they shone fierce and yellow.

At the deep-down bottom of the chasm Robin could see a black hole. Curls of menacing mist tumbled around the cavity and from the gaping mouth came such gruntings and crunchings that he was chilled with terror.

"Aileen, it's a trap!" he shouted as he crouched on hands and knees at the lip of the valley. "Aileen, listen to me! Don't go with her!"

His voice bounced off the walls of the valley and fractured into jarring echoes.

The shock of Robin's scream jolted Aileen out of her semi-trance and into panic. As she realised what was happening she began to scrape at the stony sides of the valley in an effort to escape.

"It is too late!" laughed the evil mouth. "No mortal foot can scale the walls of my Pit. Come and meet my shadow servers."

The woman grasped Aileen's shoulders with hands like steel talons and she found herself being propelled towards the dark opening and into a Pit of demons! In the blackness she could see eyes with no bodies and she could hear the hissings and slurpings of unimaginable creatures and she knew that she was being driven towards unspeakable horrors. She did not want to go into that Pit.

"Help!" she screamed as she struggled against the inhuman strength of the woman. "Somebody help me, PLEASE!" As she cried out her hand instinctively grasped the little statue round her neck.

A large shadow loomed behind Robin and blotted out the light. Over his shoulder appeared a huge hairy dog. It leaped down into the valley, scooped Aileen up in its big mouth, sprang out of the valley again and placed her, trembling but unhurt, at Robin's side. The pair stood transfixed gazing at the apparition that towered above them. It was no ordinary dog. It was a wolfhound but it stood as tall and proud as, young stallion. The massive paws were staunchly splayed on the stony ground and the huge head was held high.

A hiss as violent as air escaping from a pressure cooker erupted from the dark valley and drew all eyes back there. The woman was now standing at the opening to her black hole. Horrified, the children watched as once again she began to change. From between the white teeth a red, forked tongue flicked and darted. The beautiful face grew hideous as the skin became lumpy and scaly. The woman's body stretched and writhed and the cloak and gown merged magically into the slime-green body of a monstrous reptile. The slender fingers grew wide webs and the nails were now talons, hooked and vicious and anxious for a victim. Only the eyes remained unchanged. They were terrifying in their unaltered slitted yellowness.

A spiked tail slashed through the air and threatened to sweep the children off their feet and down into the poisonous Pit. They clung to each other in terror. A low moan throbbed above their heads and grew into a baying howl. The huge head of the wolfhound was thrown back and from the cavernous throat came a vibrating boom that stilled the air. The monster hissed and spat in defiance and then she swung her viperous tail and prepared to launch another vicious attack.

The wolfhound snarled a warning. The monster hissed and spat but she was less sure of herself now. Once again the giant dog snarled a powerful command and the tail curled back in defeat. The wolfhound bent down now before Aileen and Robin and rested his massive body on his outstretched paws. He looked at them and they knew that they too had been given an order. Obediently they climbed up on to the broad back and no sooner had they settled themselves than the wolfhound was up on his feet and prepared for take-off. Aileen looked over her shoulder. She met a pair of malevolent yellow eyes that spoke of unfinished business.

Over the rock-strewn hillside they raced and the wolfhound's feet glided far above the ground. The air rushed past the children and Robin felt that he was flying high and free. He wanted to shout out with sheer pleasure. So he did. He let rip with a great whoop of glee and he heard Aileen laugh aloud and then join in the joyous cheering.

Daintily, for a beast of its size, the wolfhound

lolloped down a gentle slope and came to rest in a grassy hollow beside a small wood. The children had a safe landing in a soft bed of moss and not a scratch had they on them. The dog shook itself and then ambled over to a rock were it lay down to rest at the feet of a seated figure.

∞ Mathgen of the High Magic ∞

"What have you brought me Cuan, Hound of the Kings? What clamour has come to disturb the peace of Mathgen?"

Robin and Aileen were by now so shell-shocked by their extraordinary experiences that the vision before them roused curiosity rather than surprise. The man seated on the rock was strange. He had the appearance of being very old with a mane of winter-white hair that met and tangled with a silvery beard. But there was around him a vitality and energy that almost sizzled.

He was dressed in a long robe the colour of lichen and from his shoulders billowed a cloak of bog-water brown. The edge of the cloak was bordered with outlandish designs that twisted and twined into brightly coloured birds and animals. In a bony hand he carried a long white rod with a knob at the top that was as clear and pure as crystal.

"Mortals," sighed the weird old man when he had studied the children at his leisure. "Whenever there is trouble you can be sure the hand of a mortal is in it somewhere. Which of you has caused the worlds to tremble?"

Robin looked at Aileen and Aileen looked at Robin. Each had been guilty of minor crimes in the past, like putting balls through windows or stealing chocolate biscuits, but never before had they stood accused of causing worlds to tremble. Aileen giggled.

"Laughter!" fumed the enraged stranger. "This mortal dares to laugh in the presence of Mathgen of the High Magic!"

Aileen and Robin didn't know what to make of this at all so they shifted from foot to foot and said nothing.

"No words?" bawled the old man. "Never in three thousand lifetimes have mortals been short of words. Which of you called to the Children of Danu for help? Speak up now or I will have Cuan deliver you back from whence you came."

The prospect of being dumped back at the mercy of the flicking tongue and slashing tail in the black Pit loosened Aileen's tongue. "Well, I called for help . . . but . . . "

"But! But! But!" the old man spluttered impatiently. "Speak up, mortal child. What exactly happened?"

Aileen stuttered and stammered at first but soon she was pouring out the story of all that had occurred right up until the moment the wolfhound had whisked them to the edge of the wood.

During the telling a worried look came into the pale blue eyes of the old man and he stroked his beard as if to calm himself.

"So you have been to the Pit of the Hell Hag." He looked at Aileen with kinder eyes. "Now tell me, what does the Morrigan want with you?"

"I d . . . d . . . don't know what you're talking about," she stuttered. "I don't know any Morrigan."

"Well she certainly knows you and I want to know why."

"Excuse me mister . . . ah . . . sir . . . " began Robin.

"I am Mathgen, Chief Druid and High Magician to the Children of Danu. You may address me as Mathgen."

"Well . . . amm . . . Mathgen," continued Robin, "just who is this Morrigan and what does she look like?"

"The Morrigan has many different shapes and forms and many different names to go with them. She is the Caileach, the ugly hag or the beautiful witch as she chooses, and she lives in the Pit of the Hell Hag. She is the crow woman who will peck your eyes out or a serpent with fangs of poison. She is a wild cat of the mountains, a giant eel that will squeeze the life from you or a worm that will crawl into your ear and devour your soul. She can divide into a cauldron of squirming maggots or become a rock in the path of the unwary. Cut off her head and it will grow back again threefold. She will trick you and possess you so that you do her evil will. That is the Morrigan, Priestess of the Fomar – the Children of the Dark. She is the essence of the Dark and her purpose is to vanquish the Children of the Light, the Danu."

During this long dramatic outburst Mathgen had paced up and down throwing his arms about like a bad actor.

"I don't think we know anyone to fit that exact description," said Robin with a perfectly straight face.

Mathgen stopped his pacing and stared suspiciously at Robin. "She has many minions in her Underworld," he said and then added ominously, "and some too in the mortal world. By what names are you known?"

When the children told him he smiled faintly and a little warmth softened the ice-cold eyes.

"Robin and Aileen. Both good names," he said. "Long known to the Children of Danu. I think you are innocents drawn into this perhaps through no fault of your own."

Then the old Druid's face grew dark and a worried frown creased his brow. "The balance is disturbed," he said sadly. "Something has caused the Morrigan to crawl out of her Pit. When Samhain comes I will be powerless against her. I fear the worst. I fear the Brod of Bres may be within her grasp."

"The Brod of Bres?" inquired Aileen politely.

"It is the Brod that keeps the balance between the powers of Darkness and the Light. If the Morrigan gains possession of the Brod she can use her Low Magic to gain dominance and wreak terrible havoc and destruction in my world and yours. Aileen and Robin, you have some part to play in this – what it is I do not know. You have been drawn into the affairs of the Otherworld, the world that was in existence long before your world began and will still be in existence when your world has destroyed itself."

"What is the Brod of Bres and where is it?" asked Robin.

"Ahh . . . " sighed Mathgen, "it is the *where* that causes me to tremble. It is such a tiny thing but mighty is its power. Since the last great battle with the Fomar it has been in the safe-keeping of the Sea-God and whilst he has it the Fomar cannot ever again make slaves of the Danu. Could Manaanan, the great God of the Sea have grown weary of his task and in a careless moment allowed the Brod to be swept from his kingdom in the depths of the Sea-River and back to the land where the Morrigan now prowls in search of it? If the Brod of Bres is loose among us then I must find it before she does!"

Mathgen had been talking almost to himself. Now he looked at the children. "Shall I tell you the story of the battle between the Children of the Danu and the Fomar and what part the Brod of Bres had to play in it?"

Without waiting for an answer he went on, "Yes, of course I shall. I am an excellent story-teller but it is a long time since I had an audience. I'm a bit out of practice and words don't flow as easily as they once did."

"You seem to be doing all right," muttered Aileen.

"Thank you," answered Mathgen bowing politely. "Let us seat ourselves here on the mossy stones and I will tell you a tale the likes of which you have never heard before."

Aileen and Robin arranged themselves as instructed and Mathgen placed himself on a stone apart from and slightly higher than the children. He folded his cloak about him and cleared his throat several times before pronouncing himself ready. Then he launched into his tale and indeed the children had never heard the likes before.

"Long ago when the Sun was young and no mortal had yet drawn breath, the Children of Danu lived to the north in Inisfail, a beautiful land of eternal light. The soil was rich and fertile and the wheat rippled yellow and the cattle grew fat. We lived under the protection of the chief god Dagda and his daughter Danu was our mother. Her love for her Children was as wide as the sky and as deep as the ocean."

The blue of the old man's eyes grew misty as he talked and his voice had a quiet haunting lilt that captured the interest of the children. Then Mathgen heaved a sigh that came straight from the soles of his sturdy sandals. A sad note now entered his voice.

"No one would want to leave such a paradise, you would think," he whispered. He seemed to have forgotten about Robin and Aileen and was now talking to himself. "But the Children of Danu were filled with curiosity and wished to see what lay beyond the Land of Light. So a fleet of stout ships was built from the finest oak trees and when we had filled them with our dearest treasures we asked our Mother Danu for her blessing before we set sail on our great adventure. Danu was not pleased. She gathered all the Gods of Light in a great Céilí and they were deeply troubled at our wish to leave Inisfail and journey to the south.

"'The land to the south is filled with the Darkness,' said our Mother Danu. 'It is the land of the Fomar. They are base people and serve base gods. Chief of these is Balor of the Evil Eye and all the peoples of the Fomar do his will. Once you have left the Land of Light you will lose the gifts I have bestowed on you. Disease and death will be your lot and you will taste evil for the first time.'

"But we did not listen. A mad fire was in our blood and a great thirst to see and learn about other worlds. And so, led by Nuada, our king, we set our ships to sail towards the sun. After many circles of the moon we came over the waters and the high waters to this land – the land we named Banba.

"Banba looked beautiful to our eyes and her people were alluring and welcoming. Could these beauteous creatures be the dreaded Fomar, the Children of the Dark and slaves of Balor? Our Mother Danu, in her anxiety to keep her Children by her side, had misled us, we thought. Where were the giants and monstrous creatures that we had been told peopled this land?

"It was a time of great celebrations and rejoicings. Many of our young men and some of our fairest maidens took spouses from among the handsome people of Banba. But the Children had not yet learned that the Fomar are shape-shifters; that they can cloak their putrid evil with countenances of exquisite beauty. We had not yet seen their slave tribes that lurk in dark caves and in hollow trees, in the dank depths of rancid lakes and in the foul waters of poisoned wells. There they await the call of their masters. When the Children of Danu had been lulled and wooed with soft music and strong wine, the trap was sprung."

At this point a sob hiccuped somewhere in the flowing white beard and the story was halted for a moment. Then Mathgen wiped a tear from the corner of his eye and continued with shaking voice.

"The Fomar rose up and showed us their true selves and monstrous was that vision. They were the power in the land and they wanted no other. Darkness and the law of Balor was their rule and they would make us slaves to his will.

"The Children of Danu were a proud people who had never known slavery and we would not bow now. Our young men were graceful and strong of limb and many a one could throw a spear as far as the midday sun or shoot an arrow into the eye of a needle. Our maidens were fleet of foot and could outstrip the fastest deer. Nuada, our king, could leap the height of the tallest mountain or wrestle a bull to the ground. But the Danu were trained to sport and hunt and had never known the battle field."

"What did you do?" whispered Aileen who twirled her hair as she listened. She was totally wrapped up in the tragic tale.

"The days of the Darkness were upon us. The Morrigan was of the Children of Danu but she was jealous of the High Magic of the Druids and was enthralled by the Low Magic of the Fomar. In exchange for the secret of their powers and for mastery over the creatures of the depths she gave her allegiance to the enemy. Once in their ranks she lusted after war and bloodshed and sought not only to lord it over the foul monsters of the Fomar but also over her own kin, the Children of the Light. She took Donn, the God of Death, as her consort and together they plotted against us.

"The battle began on Midsummer's Day and the treacherous Morrigan used her new powers to cover Banba in mists and clouds, and showers of fire and blood rained down on the Children of Danu. Before the day was out Nuada, our king, had lost his right arm in battle and many of our maidens and young men had tasted death. The Morrigan gloried in the bloodletting. As darkness fell at the end of that first day she wandered the battlefield washing herself in the blood of the fallen Danu. She continued to use her evil powers to thwart us. Our wells dried up and her magic defiled our rivers and lakes. Great flocks of carrion crows descended on our crops and devoured them. Every berry on every bush and every morsel of fish or flesh was consumed so that we faced starvation.

"I, Mathgen, Chief Druid to the Kings, called my

fellow Druids to a great Council and together we used our High Magic to break the evil spells of the Morrigan. Our warriors, male and female, were full of courage and anxious to continue the battle. But it is a law of the Danu that the king must be perfect in limb if he is to be the champion of his people and so a new king had to be chosen."

By now tears were gathering in wells in the wrinkled folds of skin beneath Mathgen's eyes and then spilling over to tumble into his beard.

"There were not many champions left among the Danu to go forward as king and when the contest was over, our new king was Bres – son of a princess of the Danu and a king of the Fomar. At the dawning of the next day of the battle, Bres led the Danu forward but treachery burned in his heart also. He too was lured by a wish to rule both Fomar and Danu and to have the slitherers in the bowels of the earth at his command. And so the base side of his nature won him over and he led the Danu towards destruction and slavery.

"Once again the Morrigan delighted in the slaughter. In her female form she fought with a sword that dripped gore, as a squawking black bird of death she hovered over the battlefield exulting in the panorama of suffering, and as serpent she slid around the feet of the Danu tripping them up or causing tall weeds to grow and choke them to death. She was triumphant and her ambition knew no bounds. Once the Danu were defeated she would possess all their powers and she would not rest until she also had the secret of the Evil Eye of Balor. The eye that contains all the wickedness that has ever been in our world and will ever be in yours."

"You were beaten then, were you?" asked Robin.

"Yes we were beaten then, Robin of the Questions," sighed Mathgen, "and our enemies made slaves of the Children of Light. Darkness had won and the evil Low Magic of the Fomar drained the power of the High Magic from the Druids and even I, Mathgen, Chief Druid to the Kings, became a hewer of wood and carrier of water. The demons of the depths now roamed the land freely and monstrous was their rule. The Morrigan was their Priestess and they obeyed her every wish."

Now Mathgen lapsed into a broody silence and although the children coughed politely to attract his attention he appeared to have forgotten them.

"Am . . . excuse me . . . " ventured Robin.

"What? What do you want? What are you doing here?" snapped Mathgen. The old Druid was so lost in his thoughts that the children no longer existed for him.

"You are nuisances," he said testily. "All mortals are nuisances. I must be off. I have more important things to do than pass time idly with interfering mortal children. Come Cuan," he shouted and he swirled about and prepared to make a grand exit into the wood.

"No!" shouted Aileen running around him and standing firmly in his path. "You can't go before you have finished the story. You can't leave us dangling like that. You must tell us what happened next!"

"Must I?" said Mathgen drawing himself to his full height and looking down imperiously at the half-fledged mortal who dared to stand in his way. His eyes flashed with cold anger and Aileen was shaken but resolute. Suddenly a smile flashed across the stern features.

"We have a bold one here," he chuckled. "Giants have grovelled before Mathgen but this little scrap of life stamps her foot and says 'Mathgen *must!*' Aileen the Fair says 'Mathgen *must!*' Very well I will give you the ending to my tale and then *I must* leave you."

∾ The Story of the Brod ∾

"For many years the Danu were slaves to the Fomar and our lot was heavy. There are none so cruel as those who turn on their own kind and Bres took pleasure in lording it over the Children of Danu. The Morrigan practised her evil arts and became more expert. With the Powers of the Darkness holding sway my High Magic was no match for hers. There seemed no escape for us."

Mathgen had resumed his epic reluctantly but now he was in full swing again. The children were again seated on the mossy stones and Aileen had cuddled up to Cuan who was resting by her side. They hung eagerly on to every word that the Druid uttered.

"The Danu are a proud people and slavery did not rest lightly on our shoulders. Secretly our smiths fashioned crude swords and spears from the broken and cast-off tools of the Fomar and our maidens and warriors practised the skills of war in hidden hollows and dark woods. Weak as we were we rose against Bres even though we were sure to be crushed in the battle. An honourable death is better than a life of slavery.

"Bres had grown lazy and careless and he was startled by the unleashed ferocity of the Danu. When a cause is hopeless people will fight to the death. The

Fomar army had lost the discipline needed for war and for a while the Danu had the beating of them.

"In her fury, the Morrigan raised all the creatures of the Underworld against us. From the lakes came the eels and the humpbacked serpents, from the sea came the Monster Muirdris, master of the lashing Tails, and from the deep caves and caverns came the crawlers and the slitherers. They turned their cruel skills on the Danu, led by the Morrigan. By her side rode Donn, his black hood thrown back so all could see his grotesque death-mask of a face. He was there with his team of black horses and his black chariot and he craved to steal our souls. His ship of death was waiting to sail to the Island of the Dead so that, even in death, the Children of Light could not rest with their Mother in the Land of Eternal Light."

"So you'd had it then," said Robin. "You couldn't fight that lot!"

"The Children of Danu did not flinch!" answered Mathgen disdainfully. "Men, aye and women too, fought with bare hands against chariot, sword and monster and the cowardly Fomar army fled before our righteous anger."

As Mathgen's story gathered speed so did he. He raced up and down shouting and slicing the air with his white stick. The children too got caught up in the excitement.

"Go on! Go on!" shouted Robin when the Druid paused for breath. "What happened next?"

"Bres roared his humiliation at his weakling warriors and so incensed was he that he beat his chest and called on Balor of the Evil Eye to come on to the battlefield and teach these fearsome slaves a final lesson.

"The calling of the gods is a serious business, not to be taken lightly. Balor lived on a wild island in the stormy Western Ocean and he was not pleased to be disturbed. All of Banba shook as his mighty foot trod the land and the Danu feared the Evil Eye that would bring final death and destruction. Balor had but one eye but it was enough. That eye possessed all the evil in the world. It had filled with poison as the child Balor watched his father brew the foul potions that corrupt minds and destroy souls. With one sweep of that eye Balor would pour out all his destructive power swamping the Children of Danu with its venom so that our skins would shrivel and pus-filled boils erupt on our bodies."

Mathgen now came to a sudden halt before the children and sat down close to them. In the manner of the master story-teller he lowered his voice to a mere whisper and the children had to strain to listen.

"Darkness filled the air and lightning flashed from the purple skies. The land crawled with reptiles and the trees filled with great black birds waiting to feed on the dead. Once again all seemed lost. The Children of Light would disappear from Banba and the Darkness would hold dominion forever."

"And was all lost?" asked Aileen breathlessly.

"Nearly," replied Mathgen. "Far off in Inisfail our Mother Danu had long watched our tribulations and sore was her heart. We had freely chosen our path and she could not interfere. But, now that Bres had called the god Balor to his side, she too could give assistance. Only gods can do battle with gods.

"The massive Balor stood astride the battlefield and fearfully we awaited the opening of the Eye. The eyelid creaked and groaned and began to shift. The Fomar cheered deliriously, certain of their victory. Suddenly the purple of the skies was tinged with a golden glow that grew and burned in a fierce light. From out of the light stepped a young boy-warrior. His yellow locks fell in profusion about his shoulders but, as yet, he had not the face hair of a man. He was armed only with a sling and a pebble."

Once again Mathgen was on his feet and once again he pranced up and down flailing his staff. "The Fomar laughed when they saw the boy step up to Balor and raise his sling. 'Is this all the Gods of Light have to offer?' they cried in derision. But the Children of Danu knew this boy-warrior and our hearts grew joyous. It was Lugh, the young God of the Rising Sun and prodigious are his powers.

"Silently we waited as the Awful Eye opened and hopefully we watched the young Lugh who did not reach the calf of Balor's iron-muscled leg. The Eye was now open and we cowered in fear. Slowly, Lugh pulled taut the thongs of his sling and aimed carefully at the ugly face. The pebble flew straight and true and pierced the gaping Eye of Balor with such force that it pushed the Eye right to the back of Balor's head."

At this Mathgen leapt in the air and gave a great whoop of triumph.

"Now the Evil Eye looked out on the Fomar and they were swept with its power. The thick hides of the reptiles and monsters split open in running sores and they crawled back into their holes to lick their wounds. The wings of the flying beasts dropped off and piled up in stinking hills of dust. The Morrigan screamed at the heavens and tore her hair in frustrated rage."

Again the Druid pranced up and down and again he brandished his staff like a sword.

"From out of a great orb of Light that now lit the skies came the Caladbolg, the magical sword that can slice through mountains. It flew into the outstretched hand of Lugh and he swung it through the air with the force of a hurricane and severed the giant head from Balor's shoulders. With the tip of the mighty blade he turned the monstrous head into stone. The petrified head he set on top of a huge mountain and there it rests even to this present day. No one knows the whereabouts of the mountain with its monstrous head and Evil Eye."

Beads of sweat were dripping down the old man's brow and he looked exhausted. He sat down and wiped his brow with the tail of his cloak.

"So, the Fomar were conquered?" said Robin.

"Oh yes indeed," smiled Mathgen. "Bres was called to account for himself and for his treachery and he too was turned into stone. But not a mighty mountain like Balor. No, Bres was turned into a tiny figure of white marble. Like Bres himself, the figure had two faces; the malevolent face of the children of Darkness and the benevolent face of the Children of Light."

The old Druid's face grew sad.

"From out of the heavens came the voice of our Mother Danu:

'My Children, you have chosen to live with the Fomar, so you must learn to live together. This Brod of Bres will keep the balance of power between Darkness and Light. I give it into the hand of Manaanan Mac Lir, the great God of the Sea-River.

Take care that your enemies do not gain possession of the Brod. It is the key that could once again open the Eye of Balor.'

At Danu's command, Lugh lifted high the tiny Brod of Bres and flung it far out over the waters. From the watery depths came the green-tinged hand of Manaanan Mac Lir and the Brod was carried deep down to his lair on the ocean floor."

Mathgen now roused himself and continued in a more matter-of-fact tone.

"After that the Fomar and the Danu divided Banba between them. The Children of the Dark went down to live in caves and caverns and we walked in the Light. The Morrigan is still the Priestess of the Underworld and she never ceases to crave total power. Nothing much has changed except the coming of mortals with their questions and seeking for answers. At first they had respect for our Magic and our gods but as time passed they became convinced that the reasoning power of the human mind is stronger than our Magic.

"So we created our Otherworld and took ourselves out of the vision of mortals. We live in our forts and our castles and tend our herds and our fields and they know not a whit about us. They believe that theirs is the only world in existence. There are some among the mortals who know about the Otherworld and the Underworld; some are our friends but some work to help the Morrigan achieve her wicked aim. And that brings me back to the start of my story. If the Brod of Bres is no longer in Manaanan's cave in the ocean depths then the Morrigan will move mountains and bend wills until she has it in her possession."

A shiver ran up Aileen's spine and she moved closer to Robin.

"So, if anybody has this Brod, they could be in danger?" asked Robin.

"Grave danger," replied Mathgen solemnly. "Now can you tell me why the Morrigan lured you to her den in the Pit of the Hell Hag?"

Robin shook his head and looked mystified. Aileen rubbed the toe of her runners on the side of her jeans and let Robin's answer serve for both of them. "Suppose someone found this Brod," she asked innocently, "what should they do with it?"

"Why bring it here to me, of course. The Brod is not the business of mortals. They are weak of mind and lack the ability to stretch beyond what they can see and understand. Now you must go. I have business to be about. It is almost Samhain and all Children of Danu must stay close to their hearths."

With that the old Druid strode majestically off into the wood with Cuan at his heels.

"Well, what did you make of that?" asked Aileen when they were alone again.

"I can't make anything of it at all," replied Robin.

"You don't believe his stories about the Underworld and the Morrigan then?"

"I don't know what to believe. I just know that when I'm with you anything is bound to happen."

The two wandered on in silence for a while and then Robin said, "Do you know the way back?"

"I think so. There is Grianan over to our right," said Aileen pointing to the hill and the ancient fort. "If we go this way we should get back to Cloughderg."

"What is this Samhain Mathgen was talking about?"

"Oh," said Aileen, "that was an old pagan feast. The people then believed that at the start of winter the sun began to die and all sorts of ghouls and ghosties wandered in the darkness. It's called Halloween now."

Again there was a silence before Robin asked another question.

"Is there something you haven't told me, Aileen?"

"What do you mean?"

"Well, do you know anything about this Brod of Bres?"

"Why should I?"

"Yes, why should you?"

The meal that evening was a cheery affair. The table was piled high with delicacies and Aileen had to admit that Aggie Scroggy was a great hand at the baking. The talk and banter flowed backwards and forwards with her mother and Rosaleen remembering childhood escapades and Hugh and Aggie telling stories that stretched far back into the past. Tom Scroggy said little – he was a man of few words – but he enjoyed himself. He sat back smiling contentedly and enjoying the crack.

Aileen too enjoyed herself and her evening was so full that she hadn't time to reflect on the happenings of the afternoon until she was alone in her room. The moon was shining in through her window so she did not put on the light. She changed into her pyjamas and then curled onto her window-sill with the curtains tightly closed. She dragged at the shoe-lace round her neck until the little white statue lay in her hand. Thoughtfully she looked at it, turning it over and over so that now one faced smiled at her and again the other scowled.

She did not doubt what she held in her hand. This was the Brod of Bres. Did it really hold the balance of power between good and evil? What would happen if the evil Morrigan did get her hands on it? And the biggest question of all – why hadn't she told Mathgen that the Brod was round her neck? Part of her wanted to believe that Mathgen was just a daft old man or maybe a figment of their imaginations. She still felt that the Brod was hers and she was loath to trust anyone. But then she remembered the yellow eyes and the three faces of the Morrigan. A sudden shiver of cold or fear sent her scuttling towards the comfort of her bed and the warmth of her duvet.

No one ever knows the exact moment they fall asleep but they can be fairly certain of the moment of awakening, especially if they are jolted from slumber. Aileen wasn't even sure that she *had* fallen asleep, but she knew that she was sitting straight up in the bed and that something had disturbed her. She held her breath and strained to listen in the black silence of the night. A sharp rattle echoed round the small room causing her heart to leap and her pulse to hammer. It came from behind the curtains that covered her tiny window. Something or someone was knocking at her window pane. Her first instinct was to stuff her fingers into her ears and huddle under the duvet but the rattle became more insistent and the glass in the pane was in danger of shattering.

Summoning all her courage, Aileen leapt from the bed and pulled back the curtains. Two yellow eyes glowed in the darkness and a blunt beak attacked the glass. The attack became more frenzied as the eyes saw the little statue that hung from Aileen's neck. She stood staring at the beast and she was so terrified that her muscles froze and she couldn't move a finger. Any moment now the glass would break and the hooded crow would invade the room to smother her with flapping wings and tear at her eyes with beak and claw!

At that precise second the room blazed with light.

"Aileen, are you all right?"

Aileen knew that the voice was Aggie Scroggy's but she was still unable to move. Strong hands gripped her shoulders and all of a sudden she felt like a rag doll. Aggie Scroggy guided her towards the bed and sat her down on the edge.

"I thought I heard a noise," the old woman said and Aileen could see that she was staring at the statue that dangled from her neck. She roused herself from her stupor and hurriedly tucked the Brod into the neck of her pyjamas.

"It was the wind rattling at the window," she said. "I'm all right now."

Aggie looked very tiny and fragile in her billowing white nightgown but Aileen didn't trust her one bit. She didn't like the way she had stared at the Brod as if she knew exactly what it was.

"I'm very tired," she said. "I want to go to sleep now." And indeed she was telling no lie. Total exhaustion had swamped her and she just wanted to sleep forever. She tumbled into her bed and turned her back to the old woman.

"I'll just fix the curtains before I leave," said Aggie and she went to the window. Aileen turned her head and out of the corner of her eye she watched. Aggie quietly slid the window up an inch or so and reached out to the sill. When she drew back her small hand it was holding something. Hurriedly she slid the object up her sleeve and then left the room turning off the light at the door. But Aileen had seen what the hand had held. It was a large, black, glossy wing feather.

Aileen knew who her night visitor had been. She also knew now that the Morrigan would give her no peace as long as she was in possession of the Brod. Her fingers curled round the little statue. She had grown very attached to it and would be sorry to part with it but she now realised that that was what she had to do. She would get up early in the morning and go and share her secret with Robin Drake. The two of them would then seek out Mathgen and the Brod of Bres would be placed where it rightly belonged – into the safe-keeping of the Children of Danu.

∾ A Plan Misfires ∾

It was impossible for Aileen to escape the next morning as early as she would have liked. When she came downstairs, still wiping the sleep from her eyes, she was astonished to find the kitchen a hive of activity. Her mother was bent over a mountainous basinful of apples, peeling and coring for all she was worth. Aggie Scroggy had her sleeves rolled up and was mixing and rolling huge sheets of pastry. A fine dust of flour hung suspended in the air.

"Oh good, Aileen," said Claire when she saw her drowsy daughter, "you can give me a hand with these."

"What are you at?" asked Aileen in astonishment.

"Apple tarts for the party in the Community Centre tonight," answered her mother. "Don't tell me you've forgotten about the Halloween party?"

Aileen had – totally.

There was no getting away then. She had to chop apples and then trim the edges and glaze the tops of endless apple tarts.

"Have you decided what you're going as?" her mother asked when the last of the bulging tarts was safely in the oven.

"What do you mean?"

"Tonight – what are you dressing up as?"

Aileen looked at her mother scornfully. "Nothing," she replied. "That sort of carry on is only for the wee ones."

"That's a pity," said Aggie. "You should enjoy yourself while you're young."

Aileen washed the tacky dough off her hands at the sink and didn't answer. "I'm going down now to Bradleys' to call for Robin," she said as she dried them on the towel at the back of the door. Her mother nodded in agreement. "I'll probably be gone for most of the day. I'll be getting something to eat in Bradleys' at lunch-time."

This was a little piece of improvisation but Aileen decided it was needed to give herself and Robin time to take the Brod of Bres to the little wood where they had met Mathgen.

Claire stared at the kitchen door as it closed behind Aileen. She was more than pleased that the girl had made friends with Robin Drake but she had a gnawing feeling that there was more going on than she knew about. She lifted her head and found her mother-in-law looking at her. Something about the old woman's eyes told her that Aggie knew something that she didn't – something not very pleasant.

Once again Rogue and the chickens scurried out of Aileen's path in the farmyard. She didn't have time to get annoyed. Now that she had decided to hand over the Brod she was anxious to get on with it. She raced down the lane towards Bradleys'. It would be good to tell her secret – to trust someone at last. As she passed the shed beside the house she heard the usual clatter and rattle of Hugh Bradley at work.

"Morning, Mr Bradley," she said putting her head

round the door. The shed was amazing. Bits of broken television sets, radios, tape recorders and coils of wire were heaped in tottering piles in every available space. Hugh was futtering at two huge speakers and around him were piled amplifiers, drums, electric guitars and keyboards. There seemed to be enough instruments and amplifiers to equip a half dozen rock bands.

"What's all this for?" she asked out of curiosity.

"They're for the hooley tonight down in the Community Centre," replied Hugh looking up from twanging an electric guitar. "Though why that crowd in Drumenny that calls itself a band needs all this stuff I'll never know. They could be just as rotten with mouth organs."

"I'm looking for Robin," said Aileen. "Is he in the house?"

"I thought it wasn't my handsome face you had come to see," grinned Hugh. "But I'm afraid you won't find Robin in the house."

"Is he out then?" asked Aileen and worry began to knot in her stomach.

"Himself and his mother were off on the early bus to Derry. Rosaleen had to get him a new overcoat or something. They should be back in the early evening."

Aileen looked so dejected that Hugh asked, "Was it something important you wanted to see him about? Do you want me to give him a message when he gets back?"

"No. Yes . . . Just say I have something to tell him. Something about yesterday."

Aileen was annoyed. She blamed everybody for her plan misfiring – Aggie Scroggy and her mother for keeping her back, and Robin Drake for gallivanting off to Derry to buy style when they had more important things to do. She wandered aimlessly down the lane wondering what to do next. If Robin didn't come back until the evening then it would be too late to go to find Mathgen and that meant she would have to keep the Brod and her secret for another night. She was quite certain she did not want to do that so she made a bold decision. She would go and find Mathgen by herself!

No sooner had she made up her mind than round the corner came Daisy chugging as she strained to climb the hill.

"Well you look as if you lost a pound and found a penny," grinned Vale from the open window of her car. Today, Vale's hair was soot black on top and the shaved hairs on the back of her head were goose-feather white. Her make-up was clown-like, with a deathly pale face, black-lined eyes and grape-black mouth. From her ears dangled red hoops big enough for a hoop-la stall. The look of her cheered Aileen.

"Hop in," said Vale. "You look as if you could do with a cup of tea and a chat."

Aileen didn't hesitate. She abandoned her newly hatched plan and jumped in beside the girl. Vale was dressed from head to toe in black. A long, loose black sweatshirt covered black leggings that stretched over firm calf muscles to meet a pair of rigidly laced black boots with heavy rounded toes and stiff slab soles. This, Aileen decided, was how she would dress if she had the saying of it.

Inside the cottage Aileen relaxed on the comfortable cushions before the open fire. She felt more at home here than anywhere else, certainly more than she did on the Scroggy farm. And she really liked Vale. She was grown-up but she wasn't like any of the grown-ups that Aileen knew. She could laugh with Vale and be herself. She could talk to her.

Vale put on a tape and gave Aileen a steaming mug of herbal tea. It smelled peculiar and tasted like mild disinfectant but to Aileen it was magic.

"Now," said Vale settling herself in the cushions, "tell me why you are looking so miserable."

Maybe it was because she was happy to see a friendly smiling face or it might have been because she had already made up her mind to tell her secret to someone – for whatever reason, she found herself pouring out her story to Vale.

The older girl sat listening in silence lapping up every word like a greedy cat at a saucer of milk.

"This Brod – have you got it with you now?" she asked when Aileen had finished. Aileen nodded.

"Could I see it?" Aileen pulled the shoe-lace and the little statue out from the neck of her jumper. Vale drew in a sharp breath of surprise.

"It's smaller than I expected," she said and then hurriedly added, "I mean from the way you described it and the great power it is supposed to have and all that, I thought it would be bigger."

"It's big enough to do a lot of damage," replied Aileen.

"Have you decided what to do about it?" asked Vale.

"Yes. I don't want to spend another night with that ugly brute of a bird tapping at my window. So I'm taking it to Mathgen – now. He will keep it safe where the Morrigan won't be able to get at it."

"I think you're very wise," said Vale as she stroked the Brod with her black painted finger nails. "But you don't have to go alone. I saw that little wood the other day. It's a good long walk away and it's started to bucket outside. We can go most of the way in Daisy. Come on – up you get."

Before she had time to think Aileen was ushered gently but firmly out of the cottage and into the car.

"It's funny," she said when she had caught her breath and they were rolling along the open road in Daisy.

"What's funny?"

"You didn't laugh at me or say I was talking stupid when I told you about Mathgen and the Morrigan and all. Most big people wouldn't have believed me."

"But then I'm not like most big people, am I?" laughed Vale and her white teeth sparkled behind the black lips. Aileen laughed too.

"Besides," continued the girl, "I wouldn't miss this for the world. It's a better story than anything I managed to get on my tape recorder since I came here." She leaned over and patted Aileen's jeans-clad knee. "I knew you were going to be a great help to me, Aileen," she grinned.

❧ Killyshee Wood ❧

Trailing round shops trying on winter jackets was not Robin's idea of a great way to spend a Saturday morning. His mother was enjoying herself though. Up and down the rails she went moving clothes backwards and forwards, holding some things up to admire and then buying nothing. Robin's thoughts were elsewhere. He still wasn't sure that yesterday had happened at all. He needed to talk to Aileen because he was convinced that she knew more than she had told either himself or Mathgen. At last his patience wore out and so he suddenly developed a blinding headache. He was in such pain that he managed to get his mother on an early bus back to Cloughderg.

"Was that all she said?" he asked his grandfather when he got home at last.

"That's it," replied his grandfather. "She just said she had something to tell you about yesterday."

"And what time was this at?"

"I suppose it was round about eleven o'clock, or maybe it was nearer twelve."

It was now nearly two o'clock in the afternoon. Robin hurried off up the lane to Scroggys'. He felt a tingle of excitement in his bones. He was sure Aileen was going to tell him something very important.

"Aileen?" inquired Aggie Scroggy who was mashing meal and potatoes in a bucket for the chickens. "She said she was spending the day with you."

"I've only just come home," said Robin. "I was in Derry. Did she not come back?"

Aggie straightened and her face looked troubled. Before she answered she walked over to the rain barrel that caught the flow from the spouting of the house, dipped her hands in the water and then wiped them dry on her apron. "No she didn't," she replied thoughtfully.

"Where would she have gone? Would her mother know?"

Aggie looked even paler than usual and Robin thought he saw fear lurking in the blue eyes.

"We'll not worry her mother for the moment," she said. "Come with me, Robin, and we'll find Aileen ourselves."

And she was off through the gate, running quickly and lightly like a young girl. She led the way down the lane and then turned off on to the track that led to the fishermen's cottages. She knocked at the door of the middle cottage and when there was no answer she lifted the latch and pushed.

Robin knew that a student who dressed weirdly and drove a daft car had moved into the cottage but he had never spoken to the girl. He followed Aggie and once across the doorstep he thought he was inside an eastern temple. The room was a blaze of colour and little bowls were smouldering quietly on window-sills and floor. He sniffed. There was a peculiar scent in the air. Aggie sniffed too.

"I thought so," she said and her face was stiff with anxiety.

"Thought what?" asked Robin.

"That smell. It was all over the house the day I came back from the field and found that girl on the doorstep. I suspected then she had been in Aileen's room. Now I know."

Robin began to poke about among the cushions and veils and soon he found a folio of drawings. They were all of two-faced stones. Did Vale Prentess know something about the Brod of Bres? His exclamation drew Aggie's attention. She looked over his shoulder.

"What have you found?"

When she saw the drawings Aggie made up her mind. "Robin," she said, and her voice was strong and determined, "Robin, you must tell me all you know. Aileen has found something important – I saw it in her room. It is strange and it worries me."

"You saw something in her room?"

"Yes. The day she came from the beach and the crow attacked her I thought something was up, something very odd. There are some of us still left who know about the crow woman and she is no friend to anybody. I knew she wasn't after Aileen for the good of her health, so I looked in her room to see what it was that Aileen had and the crow woman wanted. I saw a little statue there, a little statue with two faces. I knew immediately that, small though it was, it had great power and the crow woman wanted that power."

"The Brod of Bres," whispered Robin. "I should have known."

"Known what?" asked Aggie.

Robin was sorry he had spoken. Aileen did not trust Aggie and he knew she would be ferociously angry if he told the old woman anything. He hung his head and said nothing.

"You *must* tell me, Robin. The statue was not in Aileen's room when I took a quick look in there this morning," said Aggie. "She must be carrying it or wearing it. That means she could be in very great danger. The crow woman has allies everywhere."

And you could be one of them, thought Robin. As if reading his thoughts Aggie said, "I am not Aileen's enemy. But she *has* an enemy. Someone who spies on her and passes information on to her Mistress. That someone is Vale Prentess and Aileen is now in her clutches! Robin if you know of some way we can help Aileen you must tell me."

What was Robin to do? Who was Aileen's enemy – Aggie Scroggy or Vale Prentess? What was he to believe? He was still looking at one of the pencilled drawings and he noticed that Vale had scrawled her signature across the bottom of it. The signature began to float over the page in a crazy jumble of mixed-up letters. The image stilled. The letters came to rest and they had rearranged themselves in a new formation. Then he saw it. The name VALE PRENTESS was an anagram – an anagram for SERPENT SLAVE! He knew now who Aileen's enemy was.

Quickly he told Aggie about the meetings with the Morrigan and Mathgen. The old woman grew more and more worried as she listened. "We will have to find this Mathgen, and tell him about the Brod," she decided. "He will help us find Aileen."

Again Aggie flew down the lane and again Robin followed. "Hugh," called Aggie as she reached Bradleys' shed, "we need you and we need your van."

Hugh Bradley had just finished loading the equipment for the band into the back of his van and was about to deliver it to the Community Centre in Drumenny in time for the evening festivities. He was astonished when Aggie Scroggy and Robin came flying into his yard demanding transportation. He had never seen Aggie so agitated and he had known her long enough to know that whatever was troubling her was very serious indeed. So without a word of protest, he squeezed the two passengers into the front of the van and set off.

"I know that wood," said Aggie when Robin described where Aileen and himself had met Mathgen. "We used to call it Killyshee – the wood of the fairy mound. If we keep on the main road I'll show you where we can turn off."

They were skiting along the Drumenny Road and Hugh Bradley was still not quite sure what had happened. He knew they were looking for Aileen who had gone off somewhere with that daft young student, but that was all he knew. When they turned off the main road and on to the rough ground he complained gently.

"I hope this doesn't do any damage to the equipment in the back. I have to get it back in good condition for the Halloween party tonight."

"If we don't find Aileen there'll be no party nor anything else tonight," said Aggie and her voice was quietly urgent. Hugh Bradley looked at her. He had a great respect for Aggie Scroggy's second sight. The old woman knew many things beyond the usual. Her fear was infectious. He drove on and prepared himself to follow directions and not ask questions.

The three stood under the straggly trees at the edge of the Killyshee Wood and wondered what to do now that they were here.

"I suppose we could try calling him," said Robin and he cupped his hand over his mouth and called towards the centre of the wood, "Mathgen! Mathgen!"

Nothing happened.

"I think we should go in and look for him," said Aggie. "You stay in the van, Hugh, and keep the engine running." This sounded like a line straight from a bad gangster film but Hugh Bradley did not smile. He was happy to stay. He had no wish to leave the van and its valuable contents out here in the wilds.

Cautiously Aggie and Robin moved further into the wood where dusty shafts of daylight filtered through the high canopy of browning leaves. The floor of the wood was carpeted in a rustly riot of red and yellow leaves. When they reached what they thought to be about the centre, they found a huge moss covered boulder beside a fern-fringed pool of dark water.

"I think we are here," said Aggie. "Try calling again, Robin."

Robin searched the ground until he found a stone the full of his fist and then he banged on the boulder and shouted, "Mathgen, we know you can hear us! We have something to tell you. You must listen to us!"

He had no sooner uttered the words than a silvery thread, as fine as gossamer, began wrapping itself round him with the speed of a mad machine. Soon he was trussed up as securely as a plump fly in a spider's larder. Aggie Scroggy moved to help him but she too was stopped in her tracks. Silver threads bound her in mid stride.

"What do you want?" came a high-pitched voice

from above their heads. They looked up and there perched on the branch of a tree was a small figure. He was no taller than Robin, and as slender as a river-reed, but he was a perfectly formed adult – a miniature man. His face was smooth as a baby's but his chin was fringed with a red-gold beard. His hair was long and tied back from his face. He wore a tunic made of something soft and yellow like the chamois leather that is used for cleaning windows. Creamy wool leggings were criss-crossed below the knee with the thongs from his black boots. Across his shoulder was strapped a pouch of sorts and in his hand he held a long thin blowpipe.

"Did you do this?" demanded Robin.

"Yes we did."

This time the voice came from behind Robin and the two prisoners strained to look around. There stood another small figure. This one had no beard and the red-gold hair fell loosely about the slim shoulders. The girl, for there was no doubt that she was female, was dressed in a loose lilac-grey tunic of some flimsy material that fell to below her knee. About her waist she had a belt hung with pouched bags and on her feet she wore dainty sloe-black slippers. Although her face appeared identical to that of the little man and her cheeks had the same ruddy glow, her features were finer and she possessed a delicate beauty.

"Who are you?" asked Aggie Scroggy.

"We are the Annalaire."

The answer echoed eerily from every tree and Robin realised that the wood was peopled with many little figures – all male or female and all identical. They emerged from their camouflage and stared with open curiosity at their trussed victims.

"Are you of the Children of Danu?" asked Robin. "Did Mathgen send you?" He addressed his question to the little man who had spoken first.

"Huh!" sniffed the man disdainfully. "I am Allochar and this is my sister Cathara. These are our people. The Annalaire are nobody's children. There are more beings in the Otherworld than the Danu and the Fomar. We are the firstcomers. Our business is with the stirrings of life. Without us there would be no new buds on trees, no fresh blooms to feed the winged creatures, no clear pools to cool brows and quench thirst."

"What do you want with us?" asked Aggie.

"We want nothing to do with mortals." Cathara spoke for the first time and her voice was thin and high. "The humans poison and destroy and make us die of the ague. But we are guardians of the Threshold and under Mathgen's protection."

"It is Mathgen we have come to see. You must tell him we are here," said Robin.

"There is nothing we must do but obey the will of Mathgen. And right now he does not wish to have visitors – especially mortals."

"But he must see us," insisted Aggie. "It is very important."

"This is a very bad time," said Allochar. "At Samhain, the Danu like to stay hidden in their forts and palaces until the hours of evil have passed. Mathgen's spirits are very low, he fears the Fomar will cause trouble."

Allochar raised his slender arm and the threads that bound their bodies melted away into fine dust. "Now you must leave the wood," he said.

"We can't," said Aggie. "We have to talk to Mathgen."

"We have something to tell him about the Morrigan," added Robin.

At the mention of the evil name Cathara glided from her perch down on to the mossy boulder. Up close, Robin could see that the girl's eyes were dark purple edged with a halo of pinkish white. Her eyes were stretched wide in fear.

"You have spoken the name of All the Fears," she whispered. A rustle of unease spread through all the Annalaire in their tree perches. Allochar glided down to join his sister and he put an arm around her delicate shoulders.

"We guard Mathgen's Threshold and in return he gives us the protection of his High Magic. If we disturb him he might banish us from the Otherworld and we will die if we have to dwell in your poisoned world."

"And if you don't disturb him then the Morrigan's evil power will hold sway in both our worlds and we may all die."

Aggie's words caused the tiny twins to shiver in terror. They whispered together and then Allochar put his blowpipe to his lips and blew a reedy note that soared higher and higher until the human ear could no longer hear it. The great boulder began to tremble and pulsate with a white light that grew in intensity until it blinded the three humans and they had to cover their eyes.

"Why have I been called across the Threshold at Samhain?"

When Robin opened his eyes he saw Mathgen. The Druid seemed to have aged a thousand years since he had seen him yesterday. His body was stooped and his face was creased with anger and anxiety.

"Mortals!" he fumed when he saw them. Then he whirled on the cowering Annalaire. "You disobeyed my orders and brought me into the company of mortals!"

"We have something important to tell you," said Robin.

The old man stared at Robin and then recognition came into his eyes.

"Ah, Robin of the Questions," he said. "And where is Aileen the Fair?"

"We think the Morrigan's got her."

"And what would the Morrigan want with a mortal child? At Samhain, she has other mischief to be about."

"Aileen has the Brod of Bres."

Mathgen stared at Aggie and he seemed to be repeating her words slowly to himself. "The Brod of Bres? This mortal child has the Brod of Bres?"

"Yes," said Aggie impatiently, "and the Morrigan has the mortal child."

Mathgen now spoke to Robin.

"Did Aileen have the Brod when we spoke yesterday?"

"I think so," said Robin.

"Why didn't she tell me! Why didn't she give it to me then!" the old man wailed and he began to pace up and down leaning heavily on his staff.

"We must find the Morrigan and rescue Aileen," said Aggie.

"It is too late!" moaned Mathgen and the tears slipped down into his beard. "Already the sun is sinking in the west and the hour of the Samhain is at hand. If the Morrigan has the Brod soon she will be all-powerful. She will crush the Danu under her cruel heel."

"You have to take us to the Morrigan. We have to get Aileen away from her."

"See my hand how it trembles, and my foot how it falters," wept Mathgen. "This is the time for Low Magic. My High Magic is weak at Samhain – look." He held out his staff and Robin saw the stone at the tip had grown dim and clouded. "I know where lies the lair of the Morrigan but I am powerless against her magic."

"Take us there anyway," said Robin. "We certainly can't do anything standing around here."

"I am weak and tired. I used most of my energy coming across the Threshold. I have not the power to transport myself to the Pit of the Hell Hag."

"Then we will transport you," said Aggie taking him gently by the arm. "Can your friends, the Annalaire, get there by themselves?"

Hugh Bradley's jaw dropped open when he saw Aggie leading an ancient vision in a frock towards the van. But he pretended that there was nothing unusual about his new passenger nor the plague of overgrown midges that were swarming all over the place. He arranged the feeble old man among the drums and keyboards in the back and then settled himself behind the wheel again. "Where to now?" he asked.

"To the Pit of the Hell Hag," answered Robin.

"Right-o," said Hugh.

❧ The Pit of the Hell Hag ❧

Daisy scooted smoothly along the empty road and Aileen relaxed into a light-hearted dreamy daze. Soon the Brod would be out of her keeping and she could breathe freely. It was great being in the car with Vale. She felt grown-up and important. Vale put on a U2 tape and they sang at the tops of their voices as they whizzed along.

"I think it's somewhere here that we should leave the road," said Aileen as she struggled to remember the way to the wood where she had met Mathgen.

"Never worry yourself," shouted Vale over the loud beat of the music, "I know exactly where that wood is. I have tramped every inch of this countryside in the past couple of days. If we keep straight on and then turn right in about a mile or so we will be at the other side of it and we'll only have to walk a few yards."

Satisfied, Aileen settled herself comfortably and enjoyed the music. Ahead she could see the Grianan of Aileach silhouetted against the glowering skyline. She remembered that when she and Robin were returning from the wood yesterday they had kept the fort to their right so now the Grianan should be to their left. But when they made the turn the fort disappeared from view. The Grianan was now behind them. She pulled nervously at a strand of hair.

"Are you sure this is the right way?" she asked when Vale slid to a halt and pulled the car up on the grass verge beside a gate.

"Course it is," smiled Vale, "we'll be coming to the woods from the other side."

They climbed over the gate and found themselves in a rough field with a handful of grazing cows. The cows lifted their heads for a second and then went on with the business of chewing. They left the field by a hole in a hedge and now they were on a heather clad rising slope.

"I hope the rain stays off," said Vale. "It's getting very dirty looking."

Although it was only about three o'clock the sky had grown dark and threatening. It had been raining heavily but just now the downpour had stopped. Aileen zipped up her anorak and pulled up her hood. A mist was blowing in from the sea and she was beginning to feel very cold. They had been climbing steadily and the hillside was almost bare of heather now. The mist grew thicker and Aileen could no longer see the dark clad figure of Vale Prentess.

Around her she could hear shufflings and whisperings. The cold had grown more intense and Aileen began to shiver uncontrollably. "Vale!" she called. "Vale, I can't see you."

"Keep very still," said Vale's voice at her elbow. "I think there is something very peculiar going on."

Great swirls of mist spiralled towards them and enclosed them. Figures were moving about in the murky gloom and they seemed to be formed from the mist itself.

"What are they?" asked Aileen drawing closer to Vale.

"I don't know. Maybe they are messengers from Mathgen?"

This idea cheered Aileen – but not for very long. Out of the half-shadows emerged creatures that could only belong to the Underworld and the Morrigan. They stood on two feet as tall as men and, like humans, they had two arms, two legs and a head. But they were grotesque in shape and feature. Large bald heads were balanced precariously on scraggy necks. Each head had a snout of sorts with gaping nostrils, and a mouth grinning wide to show two rows of sharp, spiked teeth. And every head had two eyes – eyes like great globs of frogspawn with a tiny black pupil swimming in the middle. Some ears drooped to the shoulders but most were cocked, long and pointed like a hare's. Thin arms with needle-thin fingers reached almost to the ground. The bodies were pink and naked except for a covering of bristly hair. The skin hung loose over the hairy bodies and was draped in folds from scrawny shoulders to pot-bellies. Short thin legs and huge flat feet supported the ugly torsos.

The creatures began a slow shuffle forward, eyes darting and teeth grinding.

"What will we do?" cried Aileen.

"Give me your hand and trust me," said Vale.

Aileen felt herself propelled through the mist. It rolled closer now blotting out everything. She could feel the vile breath of the spectres on her face and hear their snorts but she could see nothing. The ground began to slope away until she was climbing down an almost vertical path. Stones came loose beneath her feet and rolled down into emptiness. Blindly she inched her way forward holding tightly on to Vale's strong hand.

"Easy, now," she heard Vale say, "we're almost there."

The ground had levelled out now and, guided by Vale, Aileen climbed two broad steps and then moved forward. The surface beneath her feet was now smooth and easy to walk on. Mist no longer surrounded Aileen but still she was in darkness. It was the darkness of black night on a country road. Then a blue glow shimmered and grew strong.

Shadowy figures moved in the gloom; cowled figures robed in the shrouds of death. The ghostly wraiths turned towards Aileen and beneath their hoods there was nothing – a blank, faceless emptiness. Silently the disembodied phantoms moved to flank a black and gold throne and on the throne sat the Shape-shifter in her beautiful womanly form!

"Welcome back, Aileen," said the Morrigan and her cold beauty struck terror into Aileen's heart.

"Vale," she exclaimed, "this is the Pit of the Hell Hag!"

Vale freed her hand from Aileen's grasp and said, "Yes. It is, isn't it?"

In the blue light, the pale face of Vale Prentess looked like a death mask and the black glossed lips smiled smugly.

"We have been waiting for you," said the Morrigan to Vale. "You have done well."

The realisation that she had been tricked was an awful blow to Aileen.

"Give me the Brod of Bres, mortal child."

Aileen made no move to obey the Morrigan. She was paralysed with fear and the misery of betrayal.

"You must give it to me," said the Morrigan in her low, blood-chilling voice. "The time is almost right. Soon the hour of Samhain will be upon us."

Aileen stood still.

The Morrigan raised her serpent rod and the ruby eyes flash in the dark. From behind her Aileen could hear shuffling and snorting and she knew that the creatures from the mist were in the cave and they were moving at the command of their evil mistress.

"My Skrones have not tasted mortal flesh since the Fomar were banished to the earth's innards," said the Morrigan and her yellow eyes glinted with wicked amusement. "If you do not give me the Brod then I will let them play with you. They will strip your bones clean and when they have finished I will have the Brod. But the Skrones are very slow eaters and I would prefer not to wait."

Two of the Skrones were now circling Aileen in a slow shuffle. Bulging, translucent eyes devoured her greedily and saliva slid through the spiked teeth and dripped on to pink hairy chests. From the folds of skin around the pot-bellies she could hear the rumble of anticipation. A long thin finger reached out and prodded her cheek, another poked at her stomach.

"Do I give the order, or do you give me the Brod?"

Aileen unzipped her anorak and took the Brod from around her neck. She reached the Brod into the taloned hand of the Morrigan. She really didn't have much choice.

"At last!" gloated the Morrigan as she held the little

statue aloft. "When the hour of Samhain is upon us my magic will reach the zenith of its strength. Then will I drain this Brod and transfuse all its powers to myself. I will have Mathgen's magic and all the High Magic of the Danu. The Fomar will roam free again on the earth and I will be Queen of all the Worlds. Only the supreme power of the Evil Eye will be greater than mine but I will search it out and with the Brod I will open the Eye and then none shall be my equal."

When she had finished gloating the Morrigan turned to Vale and said, "You will be well rewarded for your loyalty, my faithful servant. Now take the mortal child out of my sight and I will prepare for Samhain."

Vale shoved Aileen roughly to the side of the cave and pushed her down on a smooth stone. "Sit there and don't move," she commanded. Frantically Aileen searched the cave for an escape route. There seemed to be only one entrance and the Skrones were guarding that.

As her eyes grew accustomed to the dim light in the cave Aileen began to see things she had not noticed before. The cave was spacious with hidden recesses that throbbed with squirming life. Behind the throne was a pillar of rock standing tall and straight. The Morrigan, with her shrouded attendants following in procession, moved towards the pillar and carefully she placed the Brod of Bres on its summit. She then moved slowly round the pillar holding her rod straight out with stiffened arms and clasped hands. A fierce beam of blue-green light flowed out from the rod and encircled the pillar.

"Now it is safe," said the Morrigan when she had

completed her circle. "Only I can move through the Grumose Beam. The Brod of Bres is now beyond the reach of any being save the Morrigan."

A loud wailing chant now filled the cave startling Aileen with its sudden onslaught.

"What is happening?" she asked.

"The time of Samhain approaches," replied Vale and her grip on Aileen's shoulders tightened in excitement. "Look!"

The Morrigan had raised her rod again and the light from the reptile eyes flashed towards the ceiling of the cave. A grating sound echoed through the cavern and high up in the arched roof a circle of natural light appeared. It was the failing light of a late October evening.

"When the light fades and all is black then it is Samhain," announced Vale in a whisper, "and the Morrigan will possess the power of the Brod."

The Morrigan now prostrated herself before the Brod and the eerie chant continued. Out of the dark recesses of the cave crawled writhing reptiles, some large and slumberous, others lizard-like, tiny and darting. The armoured bodies of giant insects collided and rattled in a frenzied battle for space. The high reaches of the gloom were filled with the leathery beatings of webbed wings. All the creatures of the dark were drawn to the light of the Grumose Beam and they formed a dense circle round it and the prostrate Morrigan. The ugliness of the scene sickened Aileen.

"Every hole on the earth is filled with creatures like these," said a breathless Vale, "and more that you have not yet seen. They are all waiting – waiting for the Samhain and the triumph of the Morrigan. Once the balance of power is in her hands then they will be free. The Fomar will be masters of the worlds again."

Aileen looked up to the circle of weak daylight. It was now barely perceptible; only a purplish blush against the black roof. The chanting from the empty cowls grew more frenzied, and fierce tremors racked the body of the Morrigan. Daylight was almost gone. Within seconds it would be Samhain and then the balance of power between darkness and light would be tipped disastrously in the Morrigan's favour!

✍ A Touch of Middle Magic ✍

"Where is it then?" asked Robin. The van had rumbled over ground more rugged than any it had ever before encountered as Hugh Bradley obeyed Mathgen's instructions without question. Now the trio of mortals and the Druid of the ancient world were standing on a bleak mountainside under a darkening sky.

"It is there, beyond," said the old Druid pointing a very shaky finger.

"I can see nothing," said Aggie Scroggy. "Everything is covered in fog."

"We are at the Pit of the Hell Hag. The mist is her doing," replied Mathgen. "It is the Low Magic of the Morrigan. No one can penetrate it to reach her den."

"But you have High Magic," said Robin. "You must be able to use it to get through."

"My Magic is weak at Samhain; I cannot move against the Morrigan. I should not have left the Otherworld at this time."

"There will be no Otherworld and your Magic will never return if the Morrigan possesses the power of the Brod of Bres," said Aggie. "You have to try. You must have some strength left."

"You are right," said Mathgen, "with the Brod in her possession, the Low Magic of the Morrigan will always be stronger than my High Magic. She will seek the Evil Eye of Balor and I will be totally powerless to stop her. Then all the worlds will tremble. I *must* use every last drop of what Magic I have left to take the Brod away from her before the onset of Samhain – even if it means the end of my existence."

With a tremendous effort Mathgen drew himself to his full height and raised his white staff. He closed his eyes tightly and became very still. Then he spoke and his voice steadied and grew stronger.

"I, Mathgen, Chief Druid of the Danu, challenge the Low Magic of the Fomar."

There followed a stream of words in a language unknown to any of the others present. The white light in the stone on Mathgen's staff began to flicker rapidly and then it blazed out to pierce the thick blanketing fog. Miraculously, the fog began to shrink and soon it had disappeared completely.

But Mathgen too had shrunk. He collapsed on the ground in a shrivelled heap.

Robin ran to him. "Mathgen," he said, "are you all right?"

The old man looked about two thousand years old. His strong frame had withered and his face was criss-crossed in a pattern of deep lines and wrinkles. A fragile hand reached out and held Robin's.

"I have done what I can," came a very shaky voice. "I have no Magic left. Not even enough to take me back to my home in the Otherworld. The Pit of the Hell Hag lies at the bottom of the valley but it is almost Samhain. You possess no Magic. I fear you will be no match for the Morrigan."

The strain of talking further weakened Mathgen and he curled up like a crumpled baby and seemed to lapse into a deep sleep.

"We have to go down there," said Robin as he stood looking over the edge of the evil chasm. "We must face the Morrigan in her Pit."

"But then what do we do?" asked a bewildered Hugh Bradley. "I'm finding all of this a bit hard to swallow, but if the old man is right then we will only land ourselves in the same trouble as Aileen. We'll be no use to her at all."

"Yes," sighed Aggie, "as Mathgen says, we are only mortal. We have no magic – High or Low."

"Maybe we have," said Robin and a seed of pure genius was beginning to germinate in his brain. "Maybe we have some Middle Magic," he said and excitement bubbled in his voice. "We have the Annalaire to help us and, best of all, we have the Chief Wizard of the Middle Magic."

"What are you ranting on about Robin, what is this Middle Magic and who is this Wizard?" asked Hugh.

"You are, Granda," said Robin.

"M . . . m . . . me!" he stammered. "Would you ever talk a bit of sense, Robin."

"I *am* talking sense, Granda," insisted Robin. "Doesn't everybody around Cloughderg say you're a real wizard – a wizard with electronics?"

"Suppose so," agreed Hugh doubtfully.

"And aren't electronics *our* Magic? The magic of the human brain?"

"I think I see what you're getting at," said Aggie, her voice edged with excitement and hope. "Go on Robin," she said, "tell us what you have in mind."

"Well," said Robin, "the van is bulging with stuff. Try and think of something you can do with it, Granda.

Something that will rattle the Morrigan and give us time to rescue Aileen. I know you can, Granda."

A look of pure delight spread across Hugh Bradley's face. "You're right, me boy," he chortled. "I wonder if this Morrigan and her band of thugs have ever been to a rock concert?"

There followed a hectic half hour while Hugh did things with coils of wire and the battery of the van and Robin helped the Annalaire lower amplifiers, drum kits, key boards and synthesisers on gossamer threads that had the strength of spun galvanised steel. All the while Aggie Scroggy comforted Mathgen and urged speed as she cast worried glances at the gathering dusk.

Soon all was ready and Robin and his grandfather were huddled at the mouth of the Morrigan's cave. Inside they could hear a weird chant and the rattlings and rustlings of many bodies. Robin pulled on a pair of earphones and then he and Allochar, the Prince of the Annalaire, ventured far enough into the cave to see what was going on. It took a little while for Robin's eyes to adjust to the dim blue light in the Pit but when they did he could hardly believe what they were telling him. Many forms of life filled the spacious cave and Robin was agog at the varieties of horror on show. The fetid atmosphere caused him to retch. He steadied himself and strained to see what was happening in the cave and to try and locate Aileen.

He saw the Morrigan stretched out on the ground and the Brod of Bres surrounded by its ring of blue-green fire and then he spied Aileen. She was sitting on a stone seat and Vale was holding her tightly by the shoulders.

"Tell them to start when I raise my hand," he whispered to Allochar who was trembling by his side. Grateful to leave the evil Pit, the elfin figure flew out to Hugh and the gathered Annalaire and passed on the message. Hugh now put on his earphones and the Annalaire stopped their ears with more of their homespun threads. In the cave they saw Robin raise his hand and then Hugh Bradley switched on the equipment.

With great gusto Hugh twanged the strings of an electric guitar while hordes of Annalaire jumped on drums, cymbals and keyboards. The dreadful din filled the valley in which lay the Pit of the Hell Hag and was then channelled through amplifiers into the mouth of the cave itself. It was the most appalling noise – worse than any produced by the loudest and lousiest heavy metal band.

The explosion of sound ripped through the Pit of the Hell Hag. It startled Aileen and she stuffed her scarf into her ears and tightened the hood of her anorak. She thought at first that this was part of the Morrigan's evil ritual but then she could see that the Fomar had panicked and were beginning to stampede in an effort to escape from the ringing echoes that bounced off walls to split eardrums. Bodies were crushed or suffocated in the mad scramble. The Morrigan herself had risen to her feet and one glance at the angry contorted face told Aileen that this disturbance was not on the Shape-shifter's agenda. All was pandemonium.

Robin could see that Aileen had covered her ears and he took advantage of the noise and disorder to dart towards her. He pulled her arm to attract her attention and then slipped a pair of earphones over her head.

Then he indicated that they should both get out of there as fast as possible.

They had almost made their escape when the Morrigan spotted them. She grew to the height of a house and blocked their way. Hugh Bradley and the Annalaire saw what was happening and the shock made them cease their pounding. The silence that now filled the pit was scalding. The Morrigan looked at the two tiny figures before her and her yellow eyes were as big as satellite dishes.

To the surprise of the children, she threw back her head and laughed a great rattling hoarse cackle.

"You are clever," she chortled, "but you are too late. The hour of Samhain is come and I have the Brod of Bres. I no longer have need of you. You may go but from now on you will always be in my power."

With that the Morrigan shrank to her usual size and walked away from them towards the Brod still wrapped in the Grumose Beam. Aileen looked up at the roof of the cave and she saw that the gap was barely visible. It was almost totally dark now outside.

"It is Samhain," she said. "We need to get the Brod but I don't know how to break the Grumose Beam."

Robin realised that she was talking about the ring of green fire that surrounded the Brod. "Maybe Granda can think of something," he said and they ran to the entrance of the cave.

"These may work," said Hugh and he dug deep into the cavernous pockets of his overalls.

"They're just remote controls for the TV!" said Aileen as she saw what Hugh had thrust into her hand.

"That's right," said Hugh. "I don't know what that beam is and they're likely to be no use at all. But they're all I can think of."

"They're worth a try," said Robin. "Come on then, Aileen, we'd need to shift ourselves if we're going to rescue the Brod."

"Just stick the control into the beam, keep your fingers on the red 'Off' button and hope that the Middle Magic is still working," instructed Hugh.

"And you get back to your rock concert," said Robin nodding towards the restless monsters of the cave. "The horror film has started again."

Quickly Robin and Aileen scrambled back into the Pit of the Hell Hag. The Skrones and the other monstrous Fomar creatures were too busy trying to escape from the din that again boomed and echoed off the walls to pay any attention to them.

"I think they must be country and western fans," said Aileen as she watched their desperate efforts. But Robin didn't appreciate her humour.

The Morrigan was also too busy to notice that her enemies were once again invading her den. She was approaching the Brod of Bres and her desire for the power that it would give her made her oblivious to all else that was happening in the cave. Thus she was taken completely by surprise when a small figure darted in front of her and inserted a black object into the Grumose Beam.

To Aileen's immense delight and relief a gap appeared in the beam. She stepped into it and with her finger pressed firmly on the 'Off' button began to walk in a circle following the ring of fire. As she moved gingerly forward the beam seemed to be swallowed up by the remote control.

An agonised scream of fury rent the air and the Morrigan raised her serpent rod and pointed it towards

Aileen. The eyes flashed and another beam of light bored right through Aileen. She felt her muscles begin to petrify and her blood turn to solid ice.

"Keep on going!" shouted Robin as he jumped in front of the Morrigan. He pointed his remote control towards her rod with the serpent eyes and firmly pressed the button. The beam from the evil eyes began to expand and contract rapidly then it turned back to its source causing the rod to sizzle and flash ominously. With a yelp of pain, the Morrigan dropped the rod and the light went out.

Quickly Aileen completed her circle and then she reached up and retrieved the Brod. It was like meeting an old friend again. Before the Morrigan had time to recover Robin and Aileen had skedaddled out of the cave and back to their friends. The Morrigan stared in anguish at the opening in the roof of the cave. The sky was now completely black. Samhain had come but she had lost the Brod of Bres.

Outside it was pitch black but flashes of lightning were ripping across the sky. When the din of the impromptu rock concert had ceased, thunder could also be heard rolling in the distance but it was not loud enough to cloak the howls of the Morrigan.

When she had been hoisted out of the valley by a sophisticated system of pulleys and silk threads Aileen was surprised to find Aggie Scroggy cradling Mathgen's head in her lap. The Druid seemed barely alive. Gently Aileen prised open his gnarled hand and carefully she placed the Brod of Bres in the withered palm. Immediately the Druid's eyes flew open and he stared in amazement at the little statue. Then he began to cry.

"We are saved," he wept. "I, Mathgen, have saved all the Worlds" he declared to the amazement of the listeners. "The Morrigan is no match for Mathgen. My exploits will be regaled round every fireside when the Children of Danu gather in céilí. I alone have driven the viper from her lair!"

"So we weren't here at all then," grinned Aileen as she nudged Robin.

The strength returned rapidly to the frail body and before their eyes Mathgen was transformed to his former strapping figure. He leapt up, full of energy, and the stone on his staff was brilliant with white light. He held the staff over the valley and called out in a loud voice, "Morrigan, Goddess of War and Queen of the Fomar, my High Magic is restored and strengthened by the Brod of Bres. You will take your Low Magic and your demon slaves back to the bowels of the earth."

Immediately there was a great rumbling and shivering of rock and the entrance to the Pit of the Hell Hag began to close. The thunder exploded in a loud triumphant roar. Just before the Pit was finally sealed, a flash of lightning lit the sky and a small dark figure, with ashen face and spiked hair, could be seen squeezing out from behind a gigantic boulder. Vale Prentess, or whatever her real name was, had escaped to disappear into the blackness of the night.

"Will the Morrigan be locked in there forever?" asked Aileen.

"What is forever?" demanded Mathgen. "My High Magic is strong but even I cannot always control the Morrigan and her evil ambitions. She has her ways and means." Then he smiled comfortingly at Aileen and Robin. "But I have the Brod of Bres and the balance between Good and Evil is restored. I will take it to my World and guard it carefully. As long as it is with the Children of Danu, the Evil Eye of Balor can never be opened."

Just then the night erupted in a deafening thunder clap and the sky was ripped open in a series of lightning flashes that blinded the eyes of the mortals. When it ceased they found Mathgen on his knees with his head bent to the ground. He no longer held the Brod of Bres.

"What happened, Mathgen?" asked Aileen as she touched the Druid's trembling shoulder.

"The goddess has spoken to me," he whispered. "Danu, the Mother of the Children of Light, has spoken to her unworthy servant."

"And what did she say?" queried Robin.

Mathgen got to his feet and the children could see that he was crestfallen. "She is not pleased that the Brod of Bres is no longer in the care of Manaanan in his sea-lair and now she has delivered it into the care and protection of her Warriors who slumber under the Stone House of the Sun, the Grianan of Aileach and eternally await her call to battle. Our Mother Danu does not trust the guardianship of the Brod to Mathgen, the Chief Druid of her people."

Mathgen looked so woebegone that Aileen slipped an arm round his drooping shoulders. "Maybe it's for the best," she said. "It would be a terrible job having to keep the Brod safe from the Morrigan all the time and always having to be looking after all the Worlds as well. Now you can concentrate on being a good Druid and you can keep an eye on the Morrigan at the same time."

119

Mathgen cheered up. "You are right, Aileen the Fair," he smiled. "Our Mother Danu is very wise. It is a very important job being Chief Druid and Master of the High Magic. She knows that nothing should distract me from it."

"That's right," said Robin. "Being Chief Druid is not to be sneezed at. Didn't you save all the Worlds tonight – all by yourself?"

"Indeed I did," said Mathgen and he began to strut up and down. "I, Mathgen, the most elevated of the Children of Danu, am the saviour of all the Worlds. And I hope you mortals are properly grateful," he added with a stern look from under his bushy eyebrows.

Aileen and Robin nodded dumbly and if they were bursting to laugh, Mathgen did not seem to notice.

"I must now bid you farewell," he said, "and return to my own World."

"Well, I hope you let these boys stay for a while and help reload all my gear," said Hugh Bradley pointing to the Annalaire, "or there'll be no dancing tonight."

Aileen held her hand out in formal farewell to Mathgen. "I'll miss you," she said. "I think you are wonderful!" As the Druid took her small hand in his he puffed up with pleasure.

"I'm overcome with sadness, Aileen the Fair," said Mathgen and he snorted into a corner of his wide sleeve. "I hate goodbyes."

"Maybe it's not goodbye," said Robin. "Maybe we'll see you again sometime?"

Mathgen didn't reply. Hurriedly he tapped a rock with his staff and before he vanished into thin air the children were sure they had seen a look of pensive horror pass over his wizened face.

All the equipment had been reloaded and it was time then to say goodbye to the Annalaire.

"We did all right tonight didn't we?" said Robin to Allochar.

"We are grateful to you and your Middle Magic," replied Allochar. "We have been slaves to the Fomar before and had no wish to return to that state."

Cathara smiled at Aileen and said, "Yes. We would like to thank you in some way. Is there anything we can do for you?"

"Well," said Aileen and there was a wicked gleam in her eye, "how would you like to come to a Halloween Party?"

When all the goodbyes had been said, the four mortals piled into the van and soon they were rattling back to their everyday lives.

"We'll just about make it," said Hugh Bradley straining to look at his watch in the dark. "Do you know Robin, that this is a fancy dress affair tonight?"

Robin nodded.

"Well, I'm sure you got a few ideas for costumes from that nest of uglies back there," chuckled Hugh.

Aileen sat beside Aggie Scroggy and was very quiet and thoughtful on the journey. From under lowered eyes she peeped at Aggie. She remembered all the terrible things she had done to the old woman – and all the horrible thoughts she'd had about her. She thought of the Brod of Bres. She was just like the little statue herself. A part of her was good and a part was not so good. She had let that part get out of control. She made up her mind there and then to try harder with Aggie Scroggy and with her mother and Tom.

"Are you coming to the dance with Tom and Mammy?"

"Do you want me to come?" asked Aggie smiling in the darkness.

"Yes," said Aileen.

"Then I'll come," said Aggie.

❧ The Halloween Party ❧

Back on the Scroggy farm Tom, Claire and Rosaleen were in a right old panic. Time was wearing on and everybody seemed to have disappeared. The fate of the Halloween Dance was in the back of Hugh Bradley's van and it too was missing. A squealing of brakes heralded the return of the absentees and a tumble of tired bodies emptied on to the front yard. Rogue came leaping and barking in frantic joy to greet Aileen and when he had finished licking her face she scolded him.

"You've changed your mind, haven't you? You didn't want to know me before. What's so different about me now?"

She saw Aggie smiling and then she realised what was different – she was no longer wearing the Brod of Bres! Rogue and the other animals had sensed the presence of the little statue and its awesome power and had shied away from her.

There followed a confusion of questions and half answers that failed to satisfy but there was no time to get the whole story. Claire was glad to discover that Aileen had changed her mind about dressing up and she hurried to get white sheets for the children. Holes were cut in them and then they had their hair plastered with flour to make them look ghostly. Hugh Bradley brought two empty whiskey bottles that he used for saving coins and dangled them on strings round the children's necks.

"There you are now," he said stepping back to admire his handiwork. "Departed Spirits. What more could you ask?"

The apple cakes and barm bracks were gathered up and soon all were once again on the road and heading towards Drumenny.

Everyone from nought to ninety was going to the 'Do' in the Centre. All except the very ancient were dressed in some makeshift costume or other and all were intent on having a good time. Games, competitions and even a ghost train were organised for the children and there would be dancing – provided the band members got their equipment in time!

The main hall in the Centre looked marvellous. There were balloons and streamers everywhere and high up on a shelf that lined the walls were ghastly turnip heads with the yellow gleam of candlelight shining from grinning mouths and empty eyes. The life-size witch that had been made by the schoolchildren was suspended from the ceiling in the middle of the hall. She sat comfortably on her broom stick and her sleek black cat swayed and scowled at her squealing admirers.

Apples dangled from cords waiting for greedy mouths, and large tin baths filled to the brim with water and bobbing rosy apples were lined up in readiness for the boisterous ducking games. Long trestle tables, heavy with pyramids of fruit and mountains of nuts, propped up the back wall and there were crisps and drinks in plenty. The snooker room had refreshments too but this was off limits to children. It was a refuge for parents and elders when the noise in the hall grew unbearable.

Lambeg, who made a splendid devil with lopsided horns, forked tail and red satin cloak, was in full throttle trying to sort out the chaos – the lack of amplification was no problem to him. Mrs McCloskey, a very convincing mouse, was twittering about trying to obey his endless bellow of instructions. The Creeps, as the local band had named themselves, were prowling the stage impatiently waiting for their precious gear and they had a colourful collection of insults ready for Hugh Bradley when he finally arrived. Hugh answered with a few cheery insults of his own and set up the equipment, speedily and with his usual skill.

"Would you look at your man," whispered Aileen to Robin as she nodded to a corner at the right of the stage. The Battler Gang had assembled there and lording it over them all was a very well-fed vampire. A resplendent Battler, with hair plastered to his skull and false fangs dripping gore, was bursting out of somebody's well-worn dress suit. A cloak, hurriedly constructed from black plastic bags, was draped over his bulky shoulders.

Unfortunately the 'Departed Spirits' were spotted before they could blend into the crowd.

"Hey, there's Alien Scroggy and Sir Rubber Duck," shouted Battler as he and his cortège ambled over in their direction. "Would you look at the two wee ghosties! Wouldn't they just frighten the daylights out of a babby! You didn't use much imagination did you? I think Daffy and Donald would suit you better!"

A chorus of quacking broke out and the rest of the children were beginning to gather to see the fun. Nuala

Deery and Lisa McCarron, in gorgeous costumes, were their usual sweet selves.

"I see the whole happy Scroggy family is here, Aileen," oozed Lisa. "There's your mammy with your new daddy – real little love-birds aren't they? And there's your granny too!"

"Aye," spluttered Nuala. "Look – Aggie Scroggy's come as a witch."

"Don't be stupid, Nuala," retorted Lisa. "That's the way she always looks!" The two girls went off into screeches of helpless laughter accompanied by much back slapping and face pulling.

"Is your mammy dressed up, Chookie Birdie?" asked a sneering Ronan McCafferty as he prodded Robin with a stiff finger. "Or did she just turn her coat again?"

"Come on," said Robin with the flush of anger showing even under the layers of flour. "I'm sure we can find some nicer rats to talk to."

But the Battler was not to be deprived of his fun. He had all his cronies round him and two of his brothers, who were Creeps and built like sumo wrestlers, were watching over their 'wee' brother protectively. Robin Drake wouldn't try one of his fancy tricks here. Battler stuck out his huge boot and clamped it down on the tail of Robin's sheet. There was a ripping sound and Robin went stumbling forward and hit his head on the wall.

"You're a rotten fat coward, Battler Doherty," said Aileen angrily. "You know Robin Drake can stuff you when you're on your own."

Battler glared at her; it was for certain that her head would be next to bang off the wall.

"Right, you lot," boomed Lambeg unaware of the

hostilities, "you're holding everything up. The fancy dress parade is about to begin."

All the children in the area were shunted into line to begin the slow march round the hall. The Creeps were tuning up and attempting to play a cheerful marching tune. Aileen helped Robin to his feet.

"Our guests have arrived," whispered Robin as he rubbed a budding lump on his forehead. And there, blending in perfectly with the Count Draculas, werewolves, Ghostbusters, witches and batmen, were Allochar and his sister Cathara.

"Now the real fun will begin," said Aileen with satisfaction. "I think we should go and have a little word with them."

There was a prize of a pocket camera for the best dressed in the parade and Lisa McCarron was intent on winning it. Not that Lisa needed a camera, she had two more expensive than the one on offer, she just liked winning – especially when she had made sure she had no real competition.

Her costume was fabulous – the most expensive that money could hire. She was a frothy Fairy Godmother and her dress was sequinned and spangled and it glittered bewitchingly in the candlelight. The acres of stiff net in her crinolined skirt swirled up revealing frills and flounces and dainty satin shoes with delicate lace stockings. Lisa pranced and twirled her wand and shook her *diamanté*-crowned curls. She looked as if she had stepped straight from a Walt Disney cartoon. All the mammies gasped at her beauty and all the daddies were glad that they didn't have to fork out the price of the costume.

Round and round the parade shuffled to a dreadful

din that was supposed to be *Nellie the Elephant*. It was a bit of a farce really. Everybody knew who the winner would be. Lisa was basking in all the attention. She cast playful spells with her jewel-studded wand and smiled dimpled smiles at the entranced judges.

Then everybody saw it happening. A great big gasp of shock echoed round the hall. An impish tongue of flame darted and licked around the floating layers of dancing net! Lisa screamed and pulled at her dress. Lambeg flew into action. He rushed over to the tin baths and heaved one up on his brawny shoulders. Then he emptied the entire contents – apples and all – over a hysterical Fairy Godmother. There was a bit of pandemonium then as Lisa's weeping mother comforted her drenched daughter and her father threatened to sue everybody in sight for being insane enough to have naked flames where children could be roasted to death.

The dripping fairy was ushered off home and Lambeg and the other organisers pondered the mystery of the wandering flame. And it really was a mystery. The turnip heads were mounted high on the wall out of harm's way and when the demolished crinoline had been examined there had been no sign of any scorching whatsoever! Yet everybody in the hall had seen the curling tongue of fire. Only Robin and Aileen had seen it come from the tiny finger of a tiny hand.

The fancy dress parade continued and the eventual winner was a marvellous seven-year-old scarecrow with a carrot nose and fresh straw bursting out from the holes in his tattered suit.

The games followed next and there were great splashings and swallowings as the ducking for apples commenced. While parents' backs were turned, Battler and his pals, Willie and Ronan, amused themselves by holding heads under water until the gasping victims were almost in need of the kiss of life before they were finally released.

The Disco Dancing Competition was announced next and this was where Nuala Deery came into her own. Her body was swathed in a shiny, shocking pink leotard, boldly slashed with snaking black waves. One leg of her tights was black and the other shocking pink. She carried cheerleader pom-poms in matching black and pink and her routine was the result of trips to dancing classes in Derry and weeks of practice.

A shamble of giggling spectres lurched on to the floor and leapt and grooved to the uncertain beat of The Creeps. The judging was done by elimination and Robin and Aileen were among the first sent back to the benches. It soon became obvious that there were only two contenders. Nuala's rival was full of natural talent but she could not perform the mind-blowing well-practised antics that the vision in pink and black was producing. It isn't easy to shine on a dance floor when you're dressed as a dust-bin.

The last leg of the contest was about to begin and the band struck up. The dust-bin gyrated and did unbelievable things with her feet but all eyes were on the professional. Nuala Deery would surely have saved something special for the finale. But all was not right. Nuala was not getting into her stride. In fact Nuala was not moving at all. Her pom-poms were waving and her body was swaying but her feet were stuck fast to the floor. An anguished expression twisted her face and beads of sweat broke out on her brow but still her feet would not move.

The music stopped and the dust-bin was declared the winner. Miraculously Nuala Deery's feet could now leap and stamp in anger. She examined the floor for chewing gum and demanded a rerun but the judges were weary and anxious to get on to the next event. The Annalaire were proving very valuable guests!

Some of the adults were by now sidling off into the snooker room and others were attempting to do a quick step to the blaring of The Creeps, but Lambeg was organising the Ghost Train. This was set up in the myriad of corridors at the back of the hall and was a tribute both to Lambeg's imagination and his ability to get people do what he told them to. There he was, face as red as his cloak and enjoying himself hugely. He was lining up the children and trying to scare the eyeballs out of them with horrifying descriptions of the terrors they were about to witness.

The entrance to the train was through a door at the right side of the hall. The blacked-out tunnel then moved through corridors at the back of the Centre and out into the hall again through a door at the left-hand side. The children were a treat to terrify! They crawled in quaking relays through the tunnel and when they saw disembodied heads, half-hanged highway men and axe murderers they screamed at the tops of their lungs – even though they recognised the woman from the post office, the milkman and sometimes even their own parents. And when they came tumbling out at the other end they swore they had been within an inch of being hacked to death by grisly half-creatures.

Battler, Wee Willie and Ronan were bored. They had eaten as much apple cake as they could gorge and what fruit and nuts they could not manage to devour were stored, squirrel-like, in hidden pockets. Now they wanted a bit of excitement. The delighted squeals from the Ghost Train caught their attention. A good time was being had. They could surely put an end to that!

As luck would have it, Lambeg had gone for a well-earned cup of tea when the three desperadoes joined the ranks of shivering excited passengers for the Ghost Train. They shoved the youngsters aside and entered the tunnel in a rowdy trio and with one shared intention. They were going to destroy it. They were going to reveal all the make-believe horrors and maybe even do a bit of terrorising themselves.

The Creeps were now in full swing and, even over the din that was threatening to detonate the amplifiers, unearthly yowls could be heard coming from the Ghost Train. People looked puzzled and anxious and gradually movement halted and silence descended. The Creeps stood like players in a game of statues with mouths frozen open and limbs paralysed in action. All eyes were trained on the exit of the Ghost Train.

This was no pretend fear! The passengers on the Ghost Train were suffering unspeakable terrors if their sobbing yelps and hoarse screams were anything to go by. The whole of Drumenny witnessed the emergence of Battler Doherty, Wee Willie Clements and Ronan McCafferty from the Ghost Train and it was a sight not easily forgotten. They arrived together in a quivering heap of slobbering terror. They trembled and shook and sobbed. They grovelled and snivelled and called for mammies. They threw their arms round startled bystanders and hid their heads in surprised laps.

The sniggering started with the toddlers and soon it

grew and spread round the hall until the Battler Gang was swamped in gales of mocking laughter. They were totally disgraced. They had to be taken home by annoyed parents or, in the case of the Battler, by highly embarrassed sumo wrestlers with reputations to maintain. Later the Battler Gang claimed that they were only putting on a show for the benefit of the wee ones and people pretended to believe them. The three boys themselves had many terrible nightmares after that party. Nightmares filled with the creatures, horrible beyond human imagination, that they had met twisting and turning through the tunnel at the back of the Community Centre. Creatures that existed only in their imaginations.

After that the Ghost Train was the most popular event of the night. Grown-ups jostled with children to get to the front of the queue but they found it all a bit of a let-down. The performers, swelled by success beyond their imagination, gurgled and moaned piteously but nobody was impressed.

At the end of the night all agreed that it was the best Halloween ever. The pupils of Drumenny School had long been under the heel of the Battler Gang and fear drove them to join in their cruel sports. But they hadn't liked themselves for it. They had hugely enjoyed seeing gang members get their come-uppance and after their departure they really set about having a good time.

Aileen and Robin enjoyed themselves too. The Annalaire stayed on a little while but eventually the best sweated efforts of The Creeps sent them back to the peace and quiet of their own world. Aileen had a dance with Tom and Robin taught Aggie how to rap dance.

On the way back home Aileen was sleepy but thoughtful. An awful lot had happened to her in the past few weeks and she struggled to sort out her feelings. Tom Scroggy was all right – even a bit of a softie really and Aggie was all right too. When Aileen looked deep inside herself she found a growing respect for the old woman she once despised. She would still prefer to be living with her mother in the flat in Drumenny but her life had changed and it was not possible to turn back the clock.

Her mind turned then to the Brod of Bres and the terrors it had brought with it. She fervently hoped that it was safe now for all time, under the Hill of Grianan with the sleeping warriors.

"What are you thinking about?" asked a sleepy Robin.

"Oh, this and that."

"I wonder what it will be like back in school. Do you think the Battler Gang will leave us alone now?"

"I suppose they will for a while. But I expect they'll soon be back in action again."

"Do they still worry you?"

"Naw. How could they? Sure they're no match for a Brit and an Alien."

Also by Poolbeg

The Spirit of the Foyle

By

Mary Regan

When a hill collapses on a construction site at the Grianan of Aileach, an ancient historic site near Derry city, the Brod of Bres is once again uncovered. This little two-faced figurine has already involved Aileen Kennedy and her friend, Robin Drake, in dangerous encounters with the Morrigan, the dreaded Shape-shifter, eager to possess the mysterious powers of the Brod.

A school visit to the Tower Museum allows the children to see the Brod on display, but they also encounter an old enemy and suspect that the Morrigan has plans to steal the Brod.

Caught up in a dangerous web of intrigue the children must use all their ingenuity to outwit the power-hungry Morrigan.

When Aileen Kennedy finds a riddle in an old book given to her by Robin Drake's grandfather, her blood runs cold. She realises that the riddle could be instrumental in opening the Eye of Balor, the source of all evil. Aileen knows that the Brod of Bres, the tiny two-faced figurine she found on the beach, is the key that will open the Eye. Once opened, the Morrigan, the evil Shape-shifter, and her underworld creatures will rule.

Before the children have time to warn Mathgen, the chief Druid of the Tuatha De Danaan, the sorceress steals the riddle and soon has her hands on the Brod. The race is on – whoever solves the riddle will discover the whereabouts of the Evil Eye and learn when and how the Brod can be used to open it.

In the exciting conclusion to the Brod of Bres Trilogy, the children embark on a terrifying journey in which the forces of Light and Dark gather in one final, monumental battle.

Also by Poolbeg

Shiver!

Discover the identity of the disembodied voice singing haunting tunes in the attic of a long abandoned house . . .

Read about Lady Margaret de Deauville who was murdered in 1814 and discover the curse of her magic ring . . .

Who is the ghoulish knight who clambers out of his tomb unleashing disease and darkness upon the world?

Witness a family driven quietly insane by an evil presence in their new house . . .

What became of the hideous voodoo doll which disappeared after Niamh flung it from her bedroom window?

An atmospheric and suspense-filled collection of ghostly tales by fifteen of Ireland's most popular writers: Rose Doyle, Michael Scott, Jane Mitchell, Michael Mullen, Morgan Llywelyn, Gretta Mulrooney, Michael Carroll, Carolyn Swift, Mary Regan, Gordon Snell, Mary Beckett, Eileen Dunlop, Maeve Friel, Gaby Ross and Cormac MacRaois.

Each tale draws you into a web at times menacing, at times refreshingly funny.